P9-BBT-997

The Christmas Collection

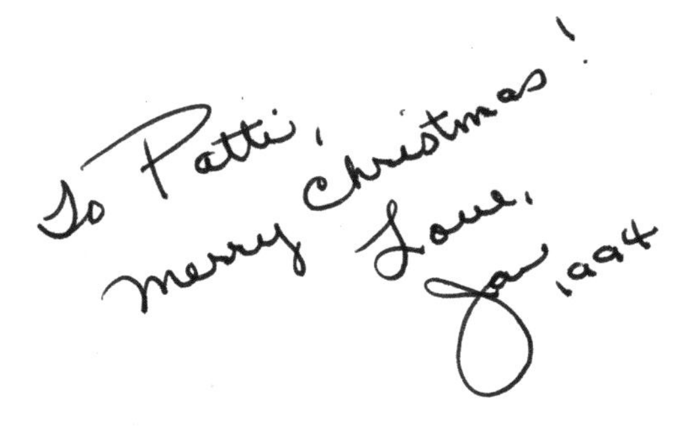

The Christmas Collection

SUSAN HILL

illustrated by

JOHN LAWRENCE

CANDLEWICK PRESS
CAMBRIDGE, MASSACHUSETTS

For Sophie
J. L.

Acknowledgements:
White Christmas commissioned 1990 by the Royal Mail
Lanterns across the Snow first published 1987 by Michael Joseph
Can It Be True? first published 1988 by Hamish Hamilton Ltd.

First U.S. edition 1994
Published in Great Britain in 1994 by Walker Books Ltd., London.

Library of Congress Cataloging-in-Publication Data
Hill, Susan, 1942-
The Christmas collection / by Susan Hill ; illustrated by John Lawrence.—1st U.S. ed.
"First published in Great Britain in 1994 by Walker Books Ltd., London"—T.p. verso.
Contents: The glass angels—White Christmas—King of Kings—Lanterns across the snow—Can it be true?
ISBN 1-56402-341-9 (reinforced trade ed.)
1. Christmas—Literary collections. [1. Christmas—Literary collections.] I. Lawrence, John, 1933- ill. II. Title.
PZ7.H5574Ch 1994 94-10511

2 4 6 8 10 9 7 5 3 1

Printed in Italy

The pictures in this book are woodcuts.

Candlewick Press
2067 Massachusetts Avenue
Cambridge, Massachusetts 02140

Contents

The Glass Angels

Chapter 1

"Wait," said Tilly, "wait. You're walking too fast."

But just as she spoke they came around the corner and out of the shelter of houses onto the sea front, and her voice was caught up on the whirl of the wind and drowned in the boom of the sea below. So her mother didn't hear her.

It was raining too, hard, cold rain like pins on their faces. For once, Tilly was quite glad that her raincoat had been somebody else's and so was too big. It came right down her legs, to meet and overlap the top of her boots, and below the tips of her fingers and almost up to her ears. Only her face and the front of her hair were getting really wet.

She stumbled, trying to keep up, and then at last her mother slowed down and shifted her bag, which was full of the pins and measuring tape, the patterns and fabric scraps and chalk, onto the other arm, so she could take hold of Tilly's hand and as she did so, she squeezed it briefly. It was a squeeze that meant a lot of things, Tilly knew. It meant understanding and friendliness and sharing Tilly's feelings about the walk home in the dark and cold and rain; it meant thank you to Tilly for sitting so long by herself on the tight-buttoned chair in Miss Kendall's back parlor and not interrupting at all while Miss Kendall was being measured and fitted and made a fuss of; it meant everything's all right and we're going home now, it's not too far and we've got one another.

So Tilly squeezed back and her squeeze meant a lot of the same things, and a few others of her own besides.

Anyway, she hadn't really minded sitting in Miss Kendall's parlor, though there had been nothing to do there except look at the row of encyclopedias, and piles of old yellow magazines about India and Africa, which were full of pictures that Tilly found either very dull or very frightening.

They had made up a fire for her and brought her a glass of milk and a fat square of gingerbread, and she had gone off into a peaceful, dreamy state, like a bird hovering on the air, not thinking, not sleeping, just breathing softly, just *being*.

The parlor was a sad room, as if no one ever went in there to talk and laugh and leave things lying around. There was a bloom of dust lying over the polish of the table, and none of the furniture quite matched, and the pictures on the walls were the kind no one ever wanted to look at, but all the same couldn't quite be bothered to get rid of.

Still, she was very used to it, visiting other people's houses with her mother, and having to sit quietly in a corner somewhere and not be a nuisance while the customer had a fitting. Very occasionally, one of them came to the apartment. But Tilly knew her mother didn't encourage that.

"My home is my home," she said.

But Tilly thought that was not the only reason. There was so little room, and most of that was full of the sewing table and the treadle machine, the tailor's dummy and the parcels of cloth, and the rail on which the half-made-up garments hung.

"People like me to fit them in their own homes, in comfort, and at their convenience," Tilly's mother said.

Which was why they were stomping home through all the wind and wet and dark of an evening two weeks before Christmas.

Christmas! As the word dropped down like a penny into the slot of her mind, Tilly slackened her steps, feeling a spurt of excitement. Perhaps, thanks to Miss Kendall, there might be something special about Christmas this year.

In the spring, Miss Kendall was to be married, and Tilly's mother was being employed to make the wedding dress and the bridesmaids' dresses, and all the clothes for Miss Kendall's going-away and her honeymoon, and that was a very good order indeed, one of the biggest her mother had ever had. It meant that there wouldn't have to be worry about the rent and the gas bill and the coal bill and the grocer's bill and Tilly's shoes, for some while. It might even mean there wouldn't be so much worry about Christmas.

But Tilly wouldn't mention that, she dared not, only hugged the thought inside her and felt a hope flickering like the coals of a small bright fire, that she would keep going herself in secret.

There was no one else walking along the esplanade. Only one or two of the street lamps were lit, and in between the pools of light those threw onto the pavement were yards and yards of darkness, like rivers they had to plunge into, Tilly thought, and cross as quickly as possible in order to reach the safety and brightness of the other side.

In the summer along here, fairy lights were strung from the trees like the colored glass beads of a necklace, and music and voices came out of the hotels and people strolled up and down enjoying the warm evening air. But no one came on a seaside holiday in December; the hotels and guest houses were closed and shuttered, though here and there, in between, was a tall house in which people lived, and a light shone from behind the curtains, making it seem more friendly.

They were walking close to the railings; once or twice Tilly put out her hand to brush against them and a chain of raindrops slid off onto her sleeve. On the other side of the railings, in the darkest of the darkness, lay the gardens, and the path that wound down and down to the seashore.

In summer there were miles of flat honey-colored sand in a curve around the bay, and the sea lay still and far out and deep blue; there were deck chairs and donkeys, buckets and spades and ice cream—and people, people, people.

How strange it is, thought Tilly, that in the middle of winter the summer seems like a dream, you can scarcely imagine it or believe it ever happened, and in the summer you sit on the hot sand in the sunshine and wonder how the winter cold and dark and emptiness could ever, ever, have been.

At the end of the esplanade, they turned and followed the curve of the road and then the sound of the sea faded, shut out by the tall houses. There were more lights in windows now, and a car went by, and a man was walking his dog; it began to feel less lonely. On the next corner, the sweet and tobacconist shop

was still open and the sweet jars gleamed and glistened like jewels in the windows. There were paper chains draped between them.

Perhaps for Christmas . . .

Past the church. Another road, with front doors set back behind long thin paths, between privet hedges and laurel bushes. Five—seven—nine—home!

They had a privet hedge, too, high and straggling, and two stone pillars guarding the gate—but down the path it was dark.

Tilly looked up at the windows. There Mr. and Mrs. Day lived, then Miss Brookes, Mrs. Plant, the Babcocks, the people with the one-eyed cat. There was no window for themselves, their attic apartment looked over the back. But while her mother dug around in her purse for the front door key and the rain ran off her collar and down her neck, Tilly was staring up at one particular window. The lamp was on and the shade of the lamp was a reddish color, so that its light glowed like the heart of a dark coal in the space where the curtains had been left slightly open. To Tilly, the light was more than a light, it was a message, a warmth, it beckoned her, it promised.

"Come inside child, do, no need to get more drenched than you already are. The clothes will take long enough to dry out as it is."

Her mother sounded suddenly weary. Tilly hopped quickly into the hall and the big door shut behind them, and they began the trudge up the five flights of stairs to the attic floor.

When they reached the second landing and saw the door at

the end of the short passage, Tilly slowed her steps, wondering, wanting, but her mother frowned, glancing back over her shoulder, and shook her head, beckoning Tilly on.

Up another. The Babcocks. Then the people with the one-eyed cat.

And then the last, short, steep flight to their own attic rooms.

By the time they reached them, of course, the lights had gone out. They always did. You pressed the switch as you entered the downstairs hall, and then you had only so long to get all the way up to the top before it clicked off again, by itself. If she ran very fast, two stairs at a time, Tilly could *just* get to their door before the light went out but her mother climbed much more slowly, especially as she was almost always carrying something, shopping or washing, or just the sewing bag.

"Why can't there be lights that stay on until you don't need them anymore?"

"Because people would forget and leave them to burn and that would cost Mr. Simpkins money."

Mr. Simpkins, the hated landlord. All the inconveniences and discomforts of their life seemed to be the fault of Mr. Simpkins—leaky faucets, drafts, the hole in the floorboard under the sink, the window that rattled, the smell on the landing, the fact that you had to stand on a chair to read the gas meter, because Mr. Simpkins was too mean to get it moved.

And the lights that never stayed on long enough.

But an hour later, everything seemed all right again. The coats had been hung up to drip over the bathtub, and the meat-and-potato pie from yesterday had heated up nicely, with a can of peas, and then Tilly had had not one but two jam tarts, because her mother hadn't wanted to eat hers.

Now she sat on the rag rug beside the fire, drinking her cocoa and enjoying the pattering of the rain on the roof and the sputtering of the gas, and the *tok-tok-tok* of her mother's scissors across the cloth rolled out on the sewing table—for there was never a time when she wasn't working. Long after Tilly had gone to bed, she would hear the sewing machine, *trundle-trundle-trundle*, sounding through her dreams.

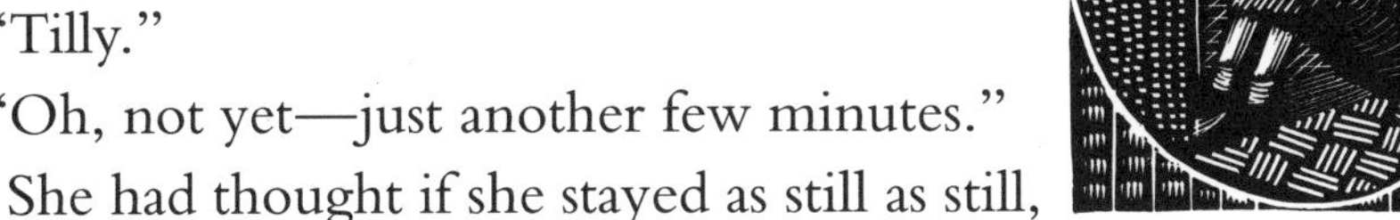

"Tilly."

"Oh, not yet—just another few minutes."

She had thought if she stayed as still as still, she might have been forgotten about, and gone to sleep here in the warmth, instead of having to uncramp herself all over again and go off into her icy bedroom.

"Tilly!" Now, there was a warning note in her mother's voice.

"All right."

She stood up. Saw the silk material, shining, creamy-white. Thought of Miss Kendall and her wedding and all the work it meant for her mother. Thought of Christmas.

Then she ran into her bedroom and turned on the washbasin faucet very, very quickly, before she had time to think about it, carrying a little of the warmth from the sitting room in with her.

When her mother came to say good night, Tilly asked, "Tomorrow after school, are we going to do a fitting?"

"No. That was the last for a while, I've just got to get on with it now. I shall be very busy, Tilly."

"Yes, I know. So please can I go down and see Mrs. McBride?"

Her mother hesitated for a moment.

"You and your Mrs. McBride."

"*Please.*"

She bent over, and tucked in Tilly's bed covers tightly.

"We'll see," she said, but in a voice that Tilly knew meant yes. "We'll have to see."

And then she went out, leaving the door just a little ajar as usual, for Tilly to see a line of light beneath it, from across the passage.

CHAPTER 2

THE NEXT SCHOOL DAY was a very good one. There was a rehearsal for the Christmas play—Tilly had only a small part, as the innkeeper's wife, but she didn't mind: she loved the whole business of standing up and speaking her line and trying on her costume, and watching the others move around the stage, loved most of all the way that, even in school clothes, everybody seemed somehow different and a little strange, part of the other world of the far, hot country and the birth of a baby in a stable, the story-play-Bible world, not the ordinary one of here and everyday.

Then, after lunch and a lesson, they had made toffee in the kitchens for the rest of the afternoon, and a lot of the toffee sugared, but it didn't really matter. They were going to wrap it up in squares of cellophane, to be sold the next week at the Christmas bazaar, along with the lavender sachets and patchwork pincushions and the fluffy balls made out of bits of yarn wound around cardboard circles

that they had been doing in needlework and handicraft all term.

But the pride of Tilly's life was the doll, Victoria Amelia, made and dressed by her own mother, with three changes of clothes, including lacy pantaloons and a tiny, fur-trimmed muff. Victoria Amelia was to be raffled. She had been held up at assembly to the whole school, and later put on display on a table in the front hall.

"Oh, Christmas, Christmas, Christmas!" sang Tilly all the way home at the end of the day.

And stopped yet again to admire the sweet jars and the chocolate figurines and the paper chains in the window of the corner shop.

"Oh, Christmas, Christmas, Christmas!"

Only the weather didn't feel very Christmassy: it was mild and muggy, and the air seemed to be heavy, to fill your lungs with water like bathroom steam, and there was a constant drizzling.

Christmas ought to be snow, snow and ice over the puddles and frost fingered into feathers on the windowpanes, and sharp, bright cold. That was how it was in books, that was how they sang it every day in the carol practices.

"Deep and crisp and even . . . "

"In the bleak midwinter . . . "

That was how it surely ought to be.

"Be careful!" her mother called out as Tilly ran up the last flight of stairs. "Be careful!" And when Tilly opened the door, she saw why.

"Oh, it's *beautiful*!"

The silk for Miss Kendall's wedding dress was unrolled over the table, and cascading down in soft, shining folds to the floor.

The chairs had been pushed back and an old clean sheet spread over the carpet.

"You'll have to eat your snack in the kitchen, Tilly. I'm sorry, I can't risk anything being spilled in here. I'll have to clear it away soon, but I do want to finish the marking-out first."

"I don't mind."

Tilly didn't; she liked to stand in the tiny kitchen that was partitioned off from the living room, and so narrow there was no space for a table or chair, just a cupboard with a worktop, beside the sink. But between the two was a space into which she could still just squeeze, and then she could stand at the long window and look out, down into the yard below, or else over the rooftops and up at the sky. Even when it was dark she liked it, liked the moonlight and the stars, and the oblongs of light from the windows below.

But tonight, the drizzle and mist made them fuzzy, and bleared the windowpane.

Tilly took her plate of bread and jam and a slab of marble cake and ate quickly, and gulped down her milk, partly because she was very hungry and school lunch hours ago, but much more because she wanted to be off, down the stairs, to knock on the magic door.

"Can I go and see Mrs. McBride?"

"If you bolt your food like that you'll get indigestion."

"No I won't, I never do."

"Now, Miss Clever . . . "

"But can I *go*?"

Her mother looked at her, resting her hand lightly on the silk.

"I'd be out of your way, wouldn't I? You could get the pattern marked out."

"Yes." A shadow of something crossed her mother's face, worry or sadness? Tilly couldn't quite tell.

Then she said, "Poor Tilly. It's a bit miserable for you, I know, always having to make way for the sewing. If we just had a bit more space . . ." She didn't bother to finish, because they both knew there was no point. Larger apartments cost more to rent and they didn't have the money.

"If I could get a few more orders like this one . . . The trouble is, I've only got one pair of hands."

And then she held one of them out, and Tilly went to her, stepping very carefully around the silk, and her mother held her, and hugged her tight for a moment.

"But I don't want to neglect you."

"You don't, I'm all right."

"Are you? Did you have a good day at school?"

"Lovely, lovely," and she told, quickly, about the play rehearsal, and the toffee-making.

"And everybody thinks Victoria Amelia is beautiful, they all want to win her."

"Well, if it makes a pound or two more."

The Christmas bazaar was to raise money for refugees who had been forced to flee their own countries during the war, and still had no proper homes. They should do whatever they could, Tilly's mother had said.

"It might have been us, Tilly. We might have been refugees if men like your father hadn't died for their country."

"Yes, I know that," Tilly said, and pulled away. She didn't like it when her mother talked like that about her father, who had been killed in the war when Tilly was a baby; it gave her a strange, hot feeling in her stomach.

She felt confused, too. A part of her knew she should be proud of her father for dying and helping them to win the war—she had been told so enough times—but another part of her was angry with him for leaving them, so that her mother had to work and work and they still had so little money and had to live in a tiny attic apartment with horrible Mr. Simpkins for a landlord. Surely it was partly his own fault: lots of other soldiers and airmen had come back home, surely he could just have been more careful not to get killed?

But these were thoughts she could never speak.

"*Please* can I go to see Mrs. McBride? You said."

"I said 'we'll see.'"

"Yes, well can we see *now*?"

Her mother laughed, and then turned back to the sewing table. "Go on, but not for too long, and if it isn't convenient for her . . . "

"I'm to come straight back. I know, I know."

And Tilly escaped, to run lightly down the flights of stairs and along the short passage to Mrs. McBride's apartment door.

It was always kept unlocked, and Tilly had agreed to a special way of knocking, so Mrs. McBride knew that it was her.

Rat-tat-tat-TAT—the first three taps the same, quite light, and the last much heavier—it was the V for Victory signal, Mrs. McBride had told her, they had played it every night on the wireless during the dark days of war.

Rat-tat-tat-TAT.

"Come in."

Whenever she opened Mrs. McBride's front door, Tilly always paused, to stand on the inner mat and close her eyes and sniff in the special and particular smell of the apartment. Most places had their own smell, their apartment smelled of material, and sewing-machine oil, the school hall smelled of polish and wood, her grandmother's house in Tenfield had smelled of coal smoke and smuts.

But Mrs. McBride's smelled of—*what* exactly? Ginger snaps,

Tilly had finally decided. Ginger snaps and violet-scented soap, mixed with a trace of candle wax, a trace of silver polish, a trace of horsehair. Altogether, it was so powerful and pleasing that Tilly liked to fill her nostrils with it the second she arrived. *I'm here*, it made her feel, *I'm really here*.

Then she crossed the hall and pushed hard against the sitting room door, so that the draft-excluder sausage moved out of the way.

Mrs. McBride was lame. She could get up and walk slowly and stiffly across the room, using her two sticks. But most of the time she stayed in her chair, which was either turned to face the window, or the fire, with her feet up on a little round beaded stool.

The room was actually quite large, much larger than their own in the attic, but Mrs. McBride had so many things crowded into it, and particularly, some very big, dark pieces of furniture, that it seemed small, and cramped. Every corner had something in it, everywhere you looked were treasures. Tilly thought she could come and sit here every day for a year and still not see everything.

In the center of the room was the great round polished table, on which stood the blue and white patterned bowl, and which had six chairs around it. Apart from Mrs. McBride's armchair, there were two others, and a deep, soft sofa, covered in cushions, round and square, large and small, cushions, embroidered, tapestried, flowered, silk, satin, velvet, wool. There were other footstools, too, one embroidered with an elephant carrying a howdah on its back, and a brown leather hassock; a tall glass-fronted cabinet against one wall filled with china ornaments and figurines, with flower-patterned plates, cups, bowls, dishes, and jugs, and another against the opposite wall displaying glass, deep, deep blue and ruby red and crystal clear. There were small tables draped with cloths

that fell to the floor, on which stood pictures in silver frames—photographs of babies in christening robes and brides in huge, flower-brimmed hats, and soldiers with medals and mustaches and an old lady with stern eyes and her hair scraped tightly back. They were all of them from Mrs. McBride's family, her mother and grandmother, her sisters, her children, her grandchildren, and her animals too, several different small dogs, and a white pony harnessed to a governess cart.

The walls that did not have the cabinets or pictures of Scottish mountains and Italian lakes had shelves with more ornaments—a set of brass monkeys, a line of eight brass bells getting smaller in size as they went down, thimbles, and three tiny enamelled clocks. By the window there was a sewing box on a stand, lined with scarlet satin, and with all the needles, threads, and buttons in special inlaid wooden trays. There were ivory lace-bobbins set out on a velvet cushion and a silver tea kettle and spirit lamp in the hearth and a fireplace screen painted over with shepherds and shepherdesses playing pipes in a woodland glade.

Beside Mrs. McBride's chair, next to the fire, were low cupboards, and inside the cupboards, more treasures, boxes filled with delights, beads and buttons, pictures sewn in silk, jewelry, old postcards, fans, a miniature set of farmyard animals, scraps of material from old wedding dresses and christening robes, lace, and a piece of ribbon that had come from an evening gown once worn by Queen Victoria.

Every time Tilly went there, Mrs. McBride would bring out a different box, and with each box came a story, some part of her past life.

Once, she had lived in a very large house, with a long drive, and a morning room, a drawing room, her own private sitting room, a breakfast room, and a parlor; there had been maids and a butler and a cook and two gardeners and a nanny, and up to ten guests to stay from Friday to Monday.

But then her husband had died and her children had grown.

"And times changed, and I rattled around that house like a marble in a bread box," she had told Tilly. So she had moved to a much smaller house.

"But one of Hitler's bombs flattened *that* and so here I am."

The bomb had set fire to the smaller house, and a lot of things had been damaged beyond repair but there seemed to have been plenty left, and all of it now crammed tightly into this sitting room, one bedroom, and a kitchenette.

"Which is plenty of space for one old woman to take up in an overcrowded world."

Now Mrs. McBride turned as Tilly came in.

"Ah, there you are. If you would please to put a speck of coal on that fire, it would look more cheerful."

So Tilly did, and scraped away some of the cinders and ash beneath with the edge of the poker so that the flames came spurting through and the coal began to crackle.

"Well, that's much brighter and better on a dark wet night. Thank you, Matilda. And how are you?"

She was the only person in the world who ever called Tilly by her full and proper name and the only one, Tilly's mother said, who would be allowed by Tilly to get away with it, for she had been Tilly from the day of her birth, to everyone—not many people even knew she was called anything different.

"But Matilda is your christened name and a good one and I had a sister Matilda," Mrs. McBride had said one day, when Tilly had first begun to come down here.

"Where is she now?"

"She died of scarlet fever at the age of two. It was a terrible thing and a great sadness."

"Children did die of things then. More than nowadays," Tilly had said.

"But never let anyone tell you it didn't matter so much, because it did. Women bore eight and lost four but every one of them was loved and grieved over, every one of them was precious."

"Like your Matilda."

"Like her."

Now, Tilly settled on the hearthrug and began to fiddle with the fringe on a blanket that was spread over the armchair, as she told about the nativity play and the carol practices and the Christmas bazaar, and the wedding dress for Miss Kendall, and as Mrs. McBride listened, her plump fingers went stiffly in and out of her crochet and her rings glinted in the firelight and the oil painting of the cavalier in the lace collar looked down at them benignly from its place above the mantel.

Later, Mrs. McBride sent Tilly for the tin in the kitchen where the marshmallows were kept, and they toasted them on a brass fork over the fire. They dissolved, sweetly, softly, stickily, in their mouths, and Mrs. McBride drank her very small glass of Madeira wine to go with them: Tilly felt herself wrapped in quietness and comfort, and warmth and contentment.

They talked of a great many things, but most of all they talked about Christmas.

"In the window of the sweet shop there are figurines made out of chocolate, wrapped in shiny paper, and marzipan snowmen, and they've hung paper chains around the jars and the grocer has boxes of Christmas crackers."

"Ah," said Mrs. McBride, "but you should have seen the windows of the big department stores before the war." Her fingers worked in and out of the crochet, and the firelight gleamed on the gold frames of her spectacles.

"Tell me," Tilly said, and tucked her legs up more tightly beneath her. She liked to hear Mrs. McBride's stories, about being a child in the country, and having grand parties in her married house. But most of all, she liked to hear about "before the war," which she always thought of as one long word. Her own mother talked about it sometimes, too. Beforethewar was a magical time, before the long dark days of bombs and blitz and blackout, of gas masks and air-raid sirens and queues and rationing and fathers gone to be soldiers.

"At Christmas, before the war," said Mrs. McBride, "when there was plenty of everything, the windows of all the big stores had tableaux—scenes from stories—fairy tales and pantomime and nursery rhymes, with models of gnomes and woodcutters and gingerbread houses and Santa Claus's workshop and elfin glades and Cinderella and Puss in Boots and Aladdin's cave and the Snow Queen and—oh, anything you could dream of, and the models moved, wheels turned and axes chopped and snowflakes fell and stars twinkled, and everything was lit from within, they all shone out into the darkness of the street; and then inside the shops the goods were piled high, the crystallized fruits and jars of ginger, and brandied cherries and plum puddings and sugared almonds and marzipan pigs, and cakes with icing and scarlet ribbons. Oh, and the toys, such toys as *you* never saw, dolls dressed in satin ball gowns and Ascot hats, and baby dolls and sailor dolls and dolls' houses with real, working lights, and dolls' prams, and teddy bears as big as ponies and lions made of real fur and clockwork trains and forts full of soldiers and farmyards full of animals and model yachts to sail on the pond. There were pineapples and figs and melons and bananas from overseas, all heaped up, and sacks of nuts and wooden boxes of dates and raisins."

"Oh, I wish it was still Beforethewar," Tilly said, looking into the fire, and trying to imagine the shops and the tableaux and the lights and the gold and silver.

"I daresay it will all come back one of these days, and more besides. But just now, Matilda, if you open my cupboard and take out the box that is tied with green string . . . I went looking in the bottom of the trunk this morning."

Mrs. McBride often "went looking in the bottom of the trunk," though it seemed to Tilly that actually the trunk didn't *have* a bottom, and must be the size of a cellar, too, so many things came out of it and there were always plenty more.

Now, she found the box, and gave it to Mrs. McBride, and then sat back on her heels, while the green string was carefully untied and rolled up into a ball and the box lid taken off.

Inside, she could see little mounds of yellowy-white tissue paper. Out came the first, then another, and another, and Mrs. McBride began carefully to unwrap each one. It took some time, and Tilly's eyes never left the box, and as she saw what was there, she felt all the old surprise and delight that came whenever Mrs. McBride found something in the cupboard, or a drawer, or opened a box or an envelope or a package; for every time it contained something beautiful or astonishing or amusing or rare or strange, and never like anything Tilly had seen before.

There had been a fan made of ostrich feathers, and a watchcase made of gold, a shawl embroidered all over with black jet beads, and a tumbling monkey and a jewel box of satin set inside a bird's egg, a wooden doll the size of a fingernail with a baby doll inside her the size of an orange seed.

"Go and switch off the big light, Matilda."

Tilly ran across the room and did so. "There now," Mrs. McBride said to her. And then Tilly turned, and looked around.

On the small table beside Mrs. McBride's chair, in the pool of light from the lamp, stood a slender column, with arms stretching out all around it like the graceful branches of a tree and the whole was made of clear crystal glass. But it might have been made of ice, Tilly thought, it glistened in just that way. Suspended from each of the branches by a silver thread as fine as a spider's skein, were angels, and the angels were made of crystal, too, with outstretched wings and haloes, and robes that were swept up into an arc at the side, and the crystal was cut into patterns all over, like the goblets in Mrs. McBride's cabinet.

And the whole thing was turning very slowly, and as it turned, the wings and haloes and outstretched robes of the angels caught the light and sparkled and glittered and the column gleamed and shone and music came tinkling from the revolving base—the music of the "Rocking Carol."

Tilly crept slowly, softly, across the room, and stood close beside the table, holding her breath for fear that the whole thing might break in pieces or vanish somehow.

"Oh, beautiful," she whispered after a while. "Oh, beautiful," and together she and Mrs. McBride watched, as the shining crystal angels turned and turned to the gentle tune, and, looking at Mrs. McBride's face, Tilly saw that she was far away from this room and this time, was somewhere else, and with other people, remembering, remembering.

CHAPTER 3

THAT NIGHT TILLY LAY IN BED, listening to the rain on the roof and, when she closed her eyes, seeing the crystal angels turning and sparkling. Her mother was still sewing, pinning up the wedding dress on the tailor's dummy. She would undress in the dark and slip into the other bed long after Tilly had gone to sleep.

But tonight, she had said that there was just one day more of work on it and then she would stop and begin to get ready for Christmas. She would come to the play and the bazaar and the carol service, and then it would be the last day of the school term, when Tilly would get out at lunchtime.

"And then, in the afternoon, we'll go shopping!"

"Can we have a tree this year, a real tree, with ornaments and silver chains, just a small one, in the corner?"

But the answer had been the usual one.

"We'll see."

There was already a fruitcake though, that had been made in October and stored away in a tin to mature. In a few days' time they would ice it.

They had spent last Christmas at Tadfield, with her mother's cousin Eleanor Flint. She had made Tilly call her Aunt Flint. It hadn't been a very happy time. Tilly's mother and Aunt Flint did not get on, and the house had been cold and polished and tidy, and there had been no decorations apart from a single line of Christmas cards on the mantelpiece.

The dressmaking business had been very slack all that year. There had been lots of the hated renovations and alterations which were more trouble than they were worth, and paid very little; Tilly's presents had been a new pair of woolen gloves, and a pencil case, and a red book of stories that had belonged to Aunt Flint when she was a girl and Aunt Flint had questioned her the whole time about what she did at school, and complained that she had "grown so" and banged doors.

"Next year, we'll stay at home. Just the two of us," Tilly's mother had said, tightening her lips, but even that, Tilly thought guiltily, did not sound very exciting.

Mrs. McBride was going to spend two days with friends; she was to be fetched by car. Tilly tried not to think of that, she did not want the lamp not to be shining through the gap in the curtains and the apartment to be empty and closed up when she went past.

"And we must take down a Christmas dinner for Miss Brookes," her mother had said the previous day. "She has no one at all in the world, poor soul. I'd ask her up here to share it with us, but she'd never manage the stairs."

Now, lying in bed, Tilly prayed that she wouldn't have to take the dinner down, as she sometimes had to take odd bits of shopping. She was afraid of Miss Brookes. Her apartment had a bead curtain in the kitchen doorway that clacked softly, and it smelled sour, and Miss Brookes talked to herself, had dirty fingernails and gypsy earrings and wild eyes and a shrieky parrot in a cage that was hardly ever cleaned out.

Her mother said she was just very lonely and neglected and rather forgetful. But Tilly always tried to get away as quickly as she could and not let Miss Brookes catch her and hold her by the arm with her hands that gripped as tight as claws.

To keep herself from thinking about it, Tilly turned over on her other side and made the picture of the crystal angels come before her eyes, and tried to remember all the things Mrs. McBride had said used to be in the shops Beforethewar. She wanted to dream about all of that, not about Miss Brookes and the terrible parrot.

The play was a great success, and at the bazaar, a girl in Tilly's class called Louisa Truman won the doll, Victoria Amelia. She was so overcome with surprise and pleasure that she grabbed Tilly around the waist and danced her all the way down the school hall, and when they got back up to the top again, out of breath, she said:

"And I want you to come to my Boxing Day party. I've told my mother and you're to ask yours. It's going to be really good, with an entertainer and an ice cream cake but you'll have to wear pumps and a party dress. Have you got a party dress?"

Tilly stood up very straight. "Yes, of course."

"That's all right then."

Though Tilly saw the look of anxiety that crossed her mother's face when she told her.

"Your party dress is from two years ago. It's much too small and I haven't time to make you another one and you don't have any pumps—would slippers do? And they live at The Uplands don't they, one of those big houses on the cliff road beyond Miss Kendall's, and there wouldn't be any buses on Boxing Day, we'd have to walk, and . . . " Her voice trailed off, but then she smiled at Tilly.

"But there, I expect we can manage somehow. If you really do want to go. I didn't know Louisa Truman was much of a friend of yours."

"Yes, she is," said Tilly quickly.

It was a lie though. She hardly knew Louisa Truman, who had only been at the school for two years, and did not really like her. She had felt a great thud of disappointment in her stomach when her name had been read out as the winner of Victoria Amelia.

The worst had been the day Louisa had called Tilly "a free place child," and lots of the class had turned around to stare.

"What is a free place child?" Tilly had demanded, bursting into the apartment that afternoon. "Am I one?"

Her mother had laid down her scissors, looking upset.

"Yes," she had said quietly. "Yes, you are. There are a few free places at your school for girls who deserve to have a good education but whose families can't afford the school fees."

"Because their fathers were killed in the war."

"Or sometimes for other reasons. It isn't anything to be ashamed of, Tilly. But I'd like to know how it got out and who it was who told you."

But Tilly had refused to say.

Now though, the thought of the Boxing Day party made her push it all down to the bottom of her mind; it shone out like a beacon. She would wear a party dress somehow, she knew her mother would manage something, and perhaps even buy her some pumps out of Miss Kendall's money, for surely she would understand that to go in furry slippers would be awful.

On the day of the carol service, Tilly's mother had a cough at breakfast that even three cups of hot tea did not soothe. She sat at the back of the church, which was very cold indeed, and Tilly could see her coughing into her handkerchief so as not to make any disturbance. On the way home, her face was flushed and her eyes oddly bright.

"I'm afraid I'm coming down with a cold, Tilly."

"Will you be better tomorrow?"

"Oh, yes, I expect so. But I think it would be a good idea if I went to bed early tonight, and had a hot drink and an aspirin. Will you be all right?"

"Of course I will."

Tilly felt important, helping her mother to bed, as if she were grown-up and in charge of things now, though inside she felt a bit uncertain. She could not remember her mother being ill like this ever before.

All that night she coughed, and the next morning she was obviously worse. When she got out of bed to go to the bathroom, she had to clutch hold of the bedhead.

"I don't think I can stand up, Tilly. I think it must be influenza—I do feel very poorly."

"What shall I do?" Tilly asked anxiously. "Should I go and tell Mrs. McBride? Shall I go to the telephone box and ring for the doctor?"

"Oh, no, no, I'll be fine. I'll just go back to sleep. I'm sure that will get me better. But you'll have to make your own breakfast and get yourself ready for school. Can you manage? And I'm afraid we won't be able to go shopping this afternoon, as I promised."

"Will you be better tomorrow?"

"Oh yes, of course."

But Tilly didn't think she sounded very certain.

The last morning of the term, and all the excitement of breaking up for Christmas lost some of its edge, as Tilly worried about her mother and wondered what would happen, what she should do. There wasn't much time left to get ready, and what if . . . She knew she ought to think just of her mother getting well, only she felt she could not bear it if, when this year Christmas had promised to be special, suddenly there was no Christmas for them at all.

She ran all the way home from the bus, through the early dark and drizzle, not even stopping to look in the window of the corner sweet shop.

Her mother seemed very ill indeed.

"Tilly, I think perhaps you *had* better ring the doctor. There's some change for the telephone in my purse. And would you go to the grocer's, we need bread and cheese and some eggs, and get a bottle of lemon barley water. I'm so thirsty."

All the time she was talking, she coughed, and her face looked shiny and damp, and her eyes seemed to have sunken into her head and gone darker.

Tilly made herself a jam sandwich with the last of the bread, and went out, eating it from her hand.

She didn't care about Christmas now, she had forgotten it, because she was frightened. Her mother had looked so ill, and her father was already dead, so what if . . . She stood stock-still in the roadway.

If her mother died, she would have no one at all, except Aunt Flint, in the cold, tidy house in Tadfield.

She began to run, clutching the coins in her hand tightly. By the time she reached the telephone kiosk, she was so out of breath she had to wait before she could speak to the person who answered at Dr. Craddock's.

"Hmm," he said, as he sat beside her mother late that afternoon, his hand on the pulse at her wrist. She was lying still now, but when Tilly had got back she had been restlessly tossing, throwing off the bed covers and muttering to herself. Once, she had half sat up and cried out and Tilly had gone in, but it was as though her mother could not see her, she stared through her somehow, before falling back on her pillows.

"Your mother is really quite ill, Tilly. I don't like the sound of her chest and she has a very high fever—she could come down with pneumonia."

Dr. Craddock looked at her intently. Tilly had known him ever since she could remember, he had treated her mumps and measles and tonsillitis and put stitches in her lip when she had fallen onto a sharp rock.

Now she saw how serious his face was and a cold feeling ran down her spine. Then he stood and beckoned her into the sitting room.

"We'll leave her to sleep."

He sat down on the arm of a chair.

"She's going to die, isn't she?" The inside of Tilly's mouth was dry, and her tongue seemed oddly big, as she spoke the words.

"Oh no, no, she won't die. But she *is* very ill and I'm concerned about you here alone—is there no one who could come and stay?"

"No, we don't have anybody."

Tilly pushed the thought of Aunt Flint away. "But I can look after her, if you tell me what I have to do."

"I was really thinking of sending her to the hospital."

"*No,* oh, please—she'd hate that, she *can't* be in the hospital for Christmas. And besides, if she did . . . "

"What would happen to you?"

"I can give her medicine and get drinks, I can help her wash. I can light the gas and make eggs on toast and come to the telephone if she gets worse—and there are people in the apartments downstairs."

"Well—that's true I suppose . . . " He waited a moment, then stood up.

"And I'll come in each day. I'll leave two bottles of medicine now, and try to make sure she has plenty to drink but otherwise, let her sleep. And if you're at all worried about anything, ring my home—have you enough coins for the telephone?"

When he had gone, Tilly went into the kitchen and stood in the window space, looking down. It was dark now, and still raining, the sound of it running down the gutters was comforting, it made her feel less alone.

But after a time, she felt afraid about things again. Her mother was sleeping. Tilly put a jug of barley water and a glass on the table beside her, and a note in case she awoke, and leaving the door unlocked, slipped downstairs.

"I mustn't stay for long," she said, standing on the hearthrug beside Mrs. McBride's chair.

And then she poured out everything, about her mother's illness that the doctor feared might turn to pneumonia, and what else that he had said, and old Mrs. McBride's hands lay still on her crochet, as she listened.

"And she won't be able to go out, and in three days it will be Christmas—only it won't, we shan't *have* a Christmas, shall we, not at all? Oh, it isn't fair, it isn't *fair.*"

Tilly cried then, not only tears of worry and fear, but of anger, too.

Mrs. McBride waited until she had quieted down.

"Well now, you'll feel much better after that. Poor Matilda, and your poor mother, too—not much of a Christmas for her, either."

"No," said Tilly, blowing her nose.

"When you've finished, go into my kitchen and look in the cupboard against the wall, to the right. You'll see a bottle of syrup."

When Tilly brought it, she said, "That mixture has cured a good many coughs and nasty chests, it will do your mother a power of good. Now—under a cloth in the larder is half an apple pie. I ate mine for lunch and your mother won't be feeling like any, but I daresay you will—put a drop of cream on it. And the third thing is over there, on the sideboard. I've been to the bottom of the old trunk again today."

It was another of Mrs. McBride's brown cardboard boxes.

"Now those," she said, "we had on the tree at my married home, every single year, and when I was a child before that. The rest were lost when the bomb fell—those are the last few left."

Carefully, one by one, Tilly took out seven Christmas tree ornaments. They felt so light and so fine in her hand, she was afraid they might break just by being touched. There were two golden and two silver spheres, on fine thread; a glistening holly-tree cone with red berries fashioned out of the glass; there was a bird with a long tail feather, peacock green and blue, and an iridescent sheen over its body that gleamed in the light, and a pointed glass star with fine silver brushwork on the tips.

"You may not be having a tree," said Mrs. McBride, "but you could surely find some place to hang them—or just set them on the windowsill to catch the light."

"Thank you," Tilly said. "Oh, they're lovely and I will be very, very careful with them."

Upstairs, she ate the apple pie with some cheese, and a piece of chocolate she found at the back of a drawer, and her mother had a drink, and a spoonful of Mrs. McBride's syrup, as well as the doctor's medicine. The syrup looked horrible, dark treacly brown and sticky and her mother said it was bitter, and puckered up her mouth in disgust at it. But before long she slept again more peacefully, though she still looked very pale, and thinner, suddenly, thinner and older.

"Tilly, are you all right, my love? What's happening about everything? Can you manage?"

But she did not wait for any proper answer, or seem to have the strength to go on worrying, just turned her head on the pillow, and closed her eyes.

Tilly put on the gas fire and sat beside it with a book in her lap. But she couldn't properly take in what she was reading and in the end she gave up and just sat, wondering. Tomorrow she thought she could go out to the shops herself to buy whatever they needed, the Christmas chicken and vegetables, and if her mother told her how, carefully, surely she would be able to cook them, and she could get fruit and perhaps some sweets. The doctor would come again, too, and then surely her mother would begin to get better? It would be all right just as long as she did not have to go into the hospital, and Tilly be sent to Aunt Flint.

But oh, it did not seem like Christmas, Tilly thought, and wished again that there might be cold and ice and snow. At least then it would look right. She went to the window again and looked out. "At least it would *feel* more like Christmas."

But there was still only the rain, more and more of it, and the darkness and the wind, so that in the end, Tilly drew the curtains tightly, and went to bed, feeling lonelier than she had ever felt in her life.

As she crossed the room, she passed close to Miss Kendall's wedding dress, cut out and tacked and pinned up on the dummy, with the cascade of silk material that would form the train, spreading out behind. Tilly touched it lightly. It felt cold, and yet warm, too, and slippery-smooth, yet with a slight roughness that caught against the pads of her fingers.

When it was finished, it would have embroidery and beading and a scalloped hem, and fine seaming at the neck and cuffs and on the bodice, and Miss Kendall would look like a bride in a picture.

Now, on the stand, the half-made dress gleamed pale and ghost-like and all at once, Tilly wished it were not there, like some silent, dead companion, and she went quickly away into the bedroom, and closed the door.

CHAPTER 4

SHE WOKE WITH A START, and sat up. Her mother was coughing again, but when Tilly called to her softly, she did not reply. It must have been the rain that had awakened her, that and the wind beating at the windows. But it seemed to her that she had heard another sound, too, a creak or a crack. Now though, there was nothing and after a while, she lay down again, and burrowed deep under the bedclothes, not so much for warmth as for comfort, the feeling of loneliness black and gnawing like hunger inside her.

When she slept again, dreams came crowding in on her, confused and peculiar and frightening, it was as though she knew she was asleep and tried to bring herself awake, but could not.

The next morning was dark, but at last, Tilly noticed, the rain had stopped. She would get up and make her mother a cup of tea. Perhaps she would be better today. Though in her heart, Tilly knew that even if she were, better would still not mean well enough for them to have a proper Christmas.

Only it did not seem to matter now, her mother's illness, coming so suddenly, had frightened Tilly, and made her feel very much alone; all she wanted was for it to be over, and for her mother to be well.

She got out of bed, and went across the passage, and opened the sitting room door, and then she gave a cry, except that the cry stuck in her throat and did not come out. She simply stood, in horror, silent and staring, staring.

There had been a long crack across the ceiling of the living room ever since Tilly could remember—a friendly sort of crack, she had somehow thought of it. But now it was not friendly at all. It was much wider, ugly and jagged and some of the plaster around it had broken away and fallen. And through the crack water, dirty water, was dripping steadily—it looked as if it had been dripping through all night, onto the tailor's dummy and Miss Kendall's white silk wedding dress and the train, and the roll of material spread out on the floor behind it. The wedding dress was quite wet and stained with dark brown, muddy stains. There was a puddle on the train, and the carpet all around was wet, too, and droppings of plaster and dirt lay on it and on the table.

Tilly knew, even in the midst of her shock and confusion and muddle, that she ought to put something under the hole to catch any more rain that might at any moment begin to fall in again, and she went to the kitchen and got a bowl, and the bucket from under the sink. But she had no idea how to begin to clear up the mess. Only whatever happened, her mother must not find out, not yet, while she was still so ill; somehow, Tilly knew she must keep it from her. It was not the ceiling that mattered, or even the carpet and the chair, it was the fact that Miss Kendall's wedding dress had been completely ruined, and Tilly had heard her mother say that the silk alone had cost forty pounds. And where would another forty pounds come from?

Then she realized, standing in the sitting room, amongst the fallen plaster and water and ruined dress, that she did not know what else to do, she could not manage alone now. Her mother being ill and Christmas in two days' time had been bad enough, but this was different.

Perhaps it was *her* fault that the plaster had fallen in, perhaps she should have noticed that something was wrong last night, a wider crack or a damp patch.

She felt muddled and troubled and frightened, but beneath all of that, which was churning up her stomach like a stormy sea, she felt oddly calm, and sure, suddenly, about what she must do first and for the best.

She went quietly into the bedroom and dressed, and then stuffed her pillow down inside her bed and pulled the covers right up. In the gray light of early morning, it might look to her mother as if she was still in bed, humped up asleep.

"Please don't let her find it," she said, an urgent, whispered-aloud prayer. "Please let her stay asleep."

And then she went, pulling on her coat and boots in the hallway, and running down all the flights of stairs in the dark, in case the click of the light switch should wake her mother. At the end of the corridor to Mrs. McBride's, she hesitated. But no, Mrs. McBride could not climb up the stairs or go out with her for help, she was an old lady, she was for visiting and talking to, telling things, and being with companionably—but for now, this was different.

The streets were quiet, curtains still drawn at windows. No one was around. It had not begun to rain again, but as the gray dawn seeped up over the sea, Tilly saw that the sky was full of great-bellied, scudding clouds, and when she turned onto the esplanade, the sea was white-flecked and dirty-looking, heaving about within itself.

She wished she had a bicycle, it seemed farther than she had remembered, and although she ran when she could, it soon gave her a stitch in her side and she was forced to slow down to a walk again.

For a short way up the last hill toward Cliff House, a small brown dog appeared out of some bushes, and ran alongside her, and Tilly felt cheered by it and wished it would keep her company all the way. But when she reached the top of the sea front road, and turned left, she saw it scampering back, answering a distant whistle.

She had never been as far as this by herself—perhaps, if circumstances had been different, she might have enjoyed it, smelling the salt on the air and feeling independent, passing the closed-up hotels and dreaming of summer, imagining. Only now she was hardly aware of her surroundings, she was simply kept going by the urgency of where she had to go, and why.

Then, she reached the great, double-fronted house, and saw a light on, and felt her heart pounding, as she scrunched and scurried up the gravel drive to the steps, and the front door.

A man opened it, a small, bald man with a mustache. He was wearing a red bathrobe.

"Well, bless me," he said, looking Tilly closely up and down. "Who in heaven's name are you?"

"I'm Tilly," she said, and then faltered, and began again.

"My name is Matilda Cumberland and please may I see Miss Kendall . . . it's . . . it's very, very important."

And then, without any warning to herself at all, she burst into tears.

Behind the man, as he brought her inside, she heard someone else, saw a woman, though not Miss Kendall.

"Good gracious, Gerald. I think it's the dressmaker's child!"

When they had been to this house before, for Miss Kendall to choose patterns and be measured, Miss Kendall's mother had been kind enough to Tilly but distant—her smile had not been the sort of smile that meant warmth and friendship, just politeness. Tilly thought they were rich and grand and snobbish, and she had not liked the way Mrs. Kendall had called her "the dressmaker's child" just now.

But whatever they thought of her, they showed only concern and helpfulness. She was taken not into the little back parlor but the dining room, where there was a fire and silver candlesticks and a Christmas tree in the window, and breakfast was set out, and they made her have hot milk with honey stirred into it and porridge with cream, and Miss

Kendall was fetched down, and sat beside her, and her hair floated loose onto her shoulders, and she looked younger and somehow softer, Tilly thought. Her brother was there too, Mr. Alec Kendall, and he waved a slice of toast at Tilly and winked, and spoke with his mouth full.

But it was hard to smile or swallow the food. She was so afraid, full of the enormity of what had happened, and the awfulness of what she had to tell them. Yet when she did, pouring it out in a great rush, somehow it was all right, in spite of the way they all sat around her and stared at her in silence as she spoke.

"And you say your mother hadn't woken up when you came out, she knows nothing of this?" asked Mr. Kendall.

"No, but she might have woken up now, I'll have to go back." She turned to Miss Kendall. "You see, the dress is completely spoiled, that's what I had to come and tell you, it's wet and covered with plaster and dirt, I don't think any of the material could be saved, and Mother said it cost forty pounds—only she doesn't have forty pounds, she couldn't buy any more, and the money she was earning for making it was going to pay the bills and—and it was for a proper Christmas, too."

She tried to swallow hard, and she dug her fingers into the palms of her hands but it was no use at all, she couldn't stop herself from crying all over again.

After that, a great many things happened, a tumble of things one after another, and in the end, Tilly just gave up and let them, because the Kendalls seemed to know best and to want to take charge and sort everything out.

Telephone calls were made, and Miss Kendall went away to get dressed, and her brother persuaded Tilly to eat a peach, and the juice ran down her chin, and he threw her his napkin to mop it up, and winked at her again. She had only tasted a peach once in her life before, and that had been in the summer, and ever after that day, Tilly was to think of rich people as the ones who had peaches to eat in December.

And then the car was brought around, and on the way home they stopped at a builder's yard, where Mr. Kendall had a talk with a man about the ceiling, and then they were swishing up through the puddles to the front of the apartment building.

"I'll go first," Tilly said, scrambling out. She had liked the car; it had smelled of leather and oil and the seats were squashy and cool against the backs of her legs.

"I'll go first in case . . . " and Miss Kendall nodded and touched her shoulder reassuringly, and Tilly saw her glance at her father, as they climbed all the stairs to the attic.

As soon as they neared the last flight, Tilly heard her mother coughing—coughing and crying.

She was sitting on the arm of the chair beside the table in her nightgown, amongst the rubble and the plaster, and the rain dripping into the bowl and bucket, and the spoiled wedding dress. For a moment, seeing Tilly, she looked frightened, and her face was as pale as the ghostly silk, but then she reached out and held onto Tilly, and could do nothing else but cry, and Tilly knelt beside her, stroking her arm and her hand. "It's all right," she said. "It's going to be all right now," and she had a strange sensation of having changed places with her mother, and done all her growing up overnight, so that she was in charge and knew what to do, and her mother was the helpless child.

The rest of the day was a confusion of comings and goings, the apartment had never been so full of so many people. The doctor came, and a builder called Mr. Rourke, and then Mr. Simpkins, their landlord, and he seemed a very different man, talking respectfully to Mr. and Miss Kendall, from the way he was with Tilly's mother. A grocer's delivery van and a butcher's boy arrived with parcels of food, and later, a nurse that Miss Kendall and the doctor had arranged for appeared, to give Tilly's mother a wash, and change her sheets, take her temperature and settle her down again on plumped-up pillows. She was actually a little better, the doctor said. While she had slept, her body had fought a battle against the infection and had begun to win; with care she would not get pneumonia now. But she was still quite ill, and must be properly looked after for at least a week.

"In the hospital?" Tilly asked anxiously.

"Well . . . " he hesitated, "she doesn't really need that now, but . . . "

"Certainly she doesn't," Miss Kendall said, "she must come to Cliff House. There are spare rooms, and the nurse can come in every day. They can spend Christmas with us."

For a moment, it seemed to Tilly that there was nothing she could do, it had all been taken out of their hands and settled, and perhaps it would be a good thing, and her mother would have a chance to get well and be properly looked after, and the Kendalls had such a beautiful Christmas tree—and peaches . . .

She sat on the sofa. Mr. Kendall had gone downstairs with Mr. Simpkins, and the builder was starting to clear up all the plaster rubble into a sack. He whistled as he did it. Tilly liked him.

"What will happen to the roof?" she asked.

"Oh, we'll patch it up and keep the old rain out for now. But next week, I'll be back to fix it good and proper." He made it sound as if it were nothing to him, just nothing at all, when Tilly had wondered this morning if the whole house would collapse, and they would have to find another apartment.

"Made a real old mess, didn't it? But things generally look worse than they are."

It was looking better already, he was right. The hole didn't seem nearly so gaping or the pile of rubble so huge.

"Will it cost a lot of money to mend?"

"Cost your old landlord a bob or two, but that's not your worry, is it?"

So Mr. Kendall really had dealt with Mr. Simpkins. Everything seemed to be running away like an express train. She ought to be glad, and grateful, and she *was,* she was . . . only . . .

"Tilly—Tilly, where are you?"

Her mother was propped up on two pillows, her hair brushed back from her face, which had just a little bit of color in it. The nurse had set out her medicines, and a jug of barley water covered with a cloth, and a sponge in a bowl, neatly on the bedside table. She would be back that evening, she had said. Tilly sat on the edge of the bed.

"Do you feel better?"

"Yes, weak, but somehow having the nurse—and knowing everything is being taken care of and that you're all right . . . "

"Yes."

"They've been very, very kind."

"Yes."

"I was so afraid when I realized you'd gone, and by yourself all that way—but you did the right thing, Tilly."

"Yes."

They fell silent, looking at one another. Then Tilly said very quietly, "Only I don't think I want to go there for Christmas."

"But Tilly—oh, love, no more do I—only we don't have anything and I couldn't go shopping—I expect it would be quite grand there—but you would have such a dull time here with me—I did get you one present but I haven't even had a chance to wrap it and—"

"But I just want to be us," Tilly interrupted, "at home. It doesn't matter about that. I don't want to go to the Kendalls, it wouldn't feel right."

"No."

There was the sound of the door then, and Miss Kendall's voice calling.

"I'll go." Tilly slid quickly off the bed. "I'll tell her."

If Miss Kendall was puzzled or offended, she did not show it, just said she understood, and made Tilly promise that she would telephone them for anything that might be needed, and said her mother was not to worry about the hole in the ceiling or the spoiled dress, but only about getting herself completely better.

"And the nurse will come in, of course, that's all taken care of," which Tilly knew meant "paid for." Only her mother said that one day she meant to pay the Kendalls back for that, because although they had been very generous and kind, it was better "not to be beholden."

At the end of the afternoon, when everyone had left, there was a bump at the door, and when Tilly opened it, Mr. Alec Kendall was there, grinning at her over the top of a huge hamper.

"Hang on," he said, setting it down on the table. "Back in a jiff."

When he appeared again, he was carrying a Christmas tree, set in a large pot.

"All in order. Good show," and he winked at her, and was gone.

Tilly walked around the tree, touching the branches here and there. It was quite bare and smelled freshly green and pungent, as though it were still growing outside. She could have Mrs. McBride's ornaments on it, and perhaps some bits of ribbon from her mother's scrap box, tied in bows.

Mrs. McBride—oh, she must see her, she must tell her everything . . . only then she remembered that Mrs. McBride would have gone away already, the apartment would be dark.

"Christmas," she said aloud to the tree, "Christmas, Christmas, Christmas."

But the room did not look like a Christmas room, and just for a moment, she wished she could change her mind and be going to Cliff House, where everything would be grand and bright and full of glitter and excitement.

Only she knew that it would not do, just as it would not do to go to Louisa Truman's Boxing Day party, where she would have felt out of place as well, and Louisa's sudden rush of friendliness toward her after winning the doll would have quite faded.

But one day, Tilly thought, standing in the window space and looking out, one day.

All the same, it was a good Christmas, very, very good, even if everything was upside-down and unexpected. The hamper had been full of treats, things they would never have had, crystallized fruits and chocolates and pears in brandy, and a pineapple and six peaches, and mince pies and marzipan animals, a ham and a tongue and a cold roast chicken, and even a little flat packet of smoked salmon, which her mother said she had not seen since long Beforethewar, and a bottle of sherry, and a tin of iced cookies.

There were some crackers, too, and some scented soaps and a decorated candle in a little china holder.

And at the bottom, in an envelope, forty pounds, in notes, to buy a new roll of wedding dress silk.

Late on Christmas Eve, they had a picnic in the bedroom, and afterward, for half an hour, Tilly's mother got up and sat in the armchair and enjoyed the tree and Mrs. McBride's ornaments, and Tilly lit the Christmas candle, and set it in the window.

As her mother was settling down to sleep, she said, "Oh, Tilly, I quite forgot—a parcel was left for you on the doormat. Miss Kendall found it."

Tilly picked up a familiar small cardboard box, tied with green string. It had an envelope slipped under it.

Dear Matilda,

My nephew will deliver this to you as we leave. I wish you both a very happy Christmas, and you are please to open this on Christmas Eve, not wait until the morning. It is for you to enjoy this year and then to keep and bring out every Christmas to come, until you are an old, old, gray-haired lady like your friend,

Christobel McBride

Tilly turned to her mother to read the letter out loud, but she saw that she was already asleep, settled on the pillow with her arm curved up behind her head. Tilly took the box and tiptoed out.

In the living room, she turned off the main light, and sitting beside the window close to the Christmas candle, she lifted out the crystal tree, with all its angels, and set it on the sill, and wound it up with the tiny golden key in the base. The window was slightly open, and a faint breeze blew in, flickering the flame of the candle, and as the angels went around, they swung a little and glinted as they caught the light and touched against each other, to make a faint ringing sound. And looking up, out of the window, Tilly saw that the rain had stopped and the clouds had parted, and there were stars pricked out in the clear sky, stars and a sliver of silver moon.

"Oh, beautiful," she whispered, "oh, beautiful," and sat, watching the crystal angels in the candlelight, until she fell into a half-sleep, half-waking trance, her head on her arm.

Every year, every single Christmas, she would watch the angels turning and hear their music, here in this room and then in other rooms she had not yet seen, on and on into the far future, until she was "an old, old, gray-haired lady."

It seemed as if she could see into that future, see the pictures of it, like the tableaux in the lighted shop windows of the past. The angels were a symbol to her of happiness to come, as they had played their part in so many happy Christmases before.

One day, Tilly thought, one day . . .

And for a while, she did fall asleep, very lightly, as she sat there.

And was awakened by the first of the midnight bells of Christmas, ringing out across the town.

White Christmas

White Christmas

It wouldn't be a white Christmas. That's what they told me. There hadn't been one for years.

I didn't say anything. But I knew.

Of course, there always used to be—so the old people in the village say.

Summers were long and hot and it always snowed at Christmas.

That's how they remember it. And the men who built our village church must have gone through some bad times too, with ice and snow for months on end.

The weather was a lot different then, they say. I sometimes think of them, hauling the great blocks of stone and chiseling them into shape, up on the tower in the teeth of a blizzard, with blue hands and faces stiff from the cold.

It always snowed for them at Christmas. And it would again this year. I just waited.

The day before Christmas Eve, the wind blew hard and the sky went gray as roof slates. We were glad to get indoors at teatime, draw the curtains and pull up to the fire. And I felt a little glow of excitement inside me, like one of the hot coals.

When I woke in the night, I knew at once. Something was different about the light and the way the air smelled. The ceiling was silvery pale.

I went to the window. Oh, and it was so beautiful! The fat white snowflakes were tumbling softly out of the sky like feathers from a goose quilt, settling on the rooftops and the church tower and the fields all around. I hugged myself for joy. A white Christmas! Just as I'd known it would be.

In the morning, the whole world was different. A new country. A magic kingdom.

At eleven o'clock, Dad and I left the kitchen, full of the warm smells of baking, and went outside. It was very bright and our breath smoked out on the air in plumes. I'd never seen the countryside look like this, softened and changed by the snow. And behind the low hills the sky was gathering again, heavy with more to come. Our boots scrunched softly as we trudged along the path leading to the church. There, beside the path, we built our snowman. He was a really good big one by the time we were done, with a scarf and an old top hat. I thought we ought to give him a stocking to hang up, too—he was one of the family now!

Later on, after lunch, we set off to fetch the Christmas tree and holly from the farm. On the way back, with the crows cawing around the bare trees and the lights going on in the houses, it was much colder and it did start to snow again. Dad said if it went on like this we'd be cut off. Back home in the warm again, we put up the tree and the green holly branches.

That night, Christmas Eve, was when I loved it best and when the snow was the most beautiful of all; then Christmas suddenly seemed to be all around us in the air, you could almost feel it. The moon had come up and we carried a lantern too, and when we began to sing the carols, people came to their windows and opened their doors to hear better and welcome us, and I felt so happy and strangely sad at the same time. "In the Bleak Midwinter" had never seemed so true.

We went around the village, singing and being given mince pies and hot drinks, and everyone was so cheerful and friendly, and I hoped it would never end.

Only, quite suddenly, I was tired and my head swam and a warm bed seemed a great place. But I wasn't too tired to hang up my stocking! Or to stand at my window for a moment in the darkness, looking out at the night sky, the stars, and the moonlight on the pale snow.

After that, Christmas somehow became a great, happy blur, of presents and people arriving and laughter, hot turkey, and roasting chestnuts and the crackling fire, and the snow was part of it all.

On Christmas afternoon and Boxing Day, everybody was out, and, on the slopes around, we tobogganed, whooshing down and tumbling off into the snow and lugging the sleds back up to the top, over and over again. There was the sound of voices calling and laughing all around the fields, and then someone said the pond

was frozen hard over, so we all went to see, and people brought out skates and there was the zip and hiss of the blades across the ice and bright scarves and hats and new sweaters, as we whirled around and around in the late afternoon light.

And the whole time, I was remembering it to tell them when I was very old, just as people had always told me. When we were young, they said, summers were long and hot and it always snowed at Christmas. It doesn't happen nowadays, they said. But it did. It snowed at Christmas that year. Just as I'd known it would.

KING OF KINGS

King of Kings

Mr. Hegarty hadn't always been alone. And being alone didn't always mean being lonely. But quite often it did.

Once, there had been Mrs. Hegarty, whose name had been Doll, or sometimes Dolly, and they had been married for a great many years, and there had been good days and bad days but mostly good, some ups and some downs, but mostly ups, and the great many years had not seemed nearly enough before Mrs. Hegarty got ill and then very much iller, and died. So that now there was only Mr. Hegarty and Cat the cat, and Jacko.

Cat the cat had never been bought or in any other way chosen, he had just come—one day onto the wall, the next day in the yard, the third day into the house, and after that, as Mr. Hegarty said, paws under the table for good.

Cat, like all cats, came and went as he pleased. But Jacko had been chosen all right, for his black-patch eye and his brave, bright bark, and for being cheap from the man with the cart in the lane, because his legs were bandy.

Mr. Hegarty's house was the last in the street. After it came the wharves and warehouses, the empty lot and the church, the building site, the road, and the railway.

But walk another way and there were still a few streets left. Though not the street where Mr. Hegarty was born and grew to be a man, nor the one where Mrs. Hegarty had been born and got married from, all those years ago. They are gone, and their neighbors' houses too, and the pub and the shop on the corner, pulled down in heaps of dust and rubble and carted away on trucks.

There were cranes now, and site offices, concrete girders and craters in the ground, men in hard hats and machines, judder-judder, all day, all day.

But walk a bit farther still, which Mr. Hegarty and Jacko always did, and there was the lane, just as it had always been, and the streets and squares around it, and shops and buses and flats and people, schools and churches, the bit of park and the King's Hospital.

And now it was Christmas Eve. Mr. Hegarty had been about all day. He liked to be about. He liked Christmas Eve. Everybody talked to everybody else and there was a lot of bustle; people were cheerful. He'd been about the market, among the stalls and carts. Then, he and Jacko had stood for a long time on the corner, just for the pleasure of watching everything. He'd had his dinner out—pie and chips—and his tea, with a mince pie "on the house." Lotta, who kept the café, had said, "because ees Christmas."

But now it was late. Dark. Now, everything was closing down. They were sweeping up around the carts, sprigs of holly and paper from the oranges and a few lost Brussels sprouts.

"Good night then. Happy Christmas."

Lamps out. Blinds up. Shutters down.

The main road was jammed. The trains went along the line, full of everyone going home. So Mr. Hegarty and Jacko went home too. Across the building site. Quiet now, the great crane still and silent. It had a Christmas tree balanced on the very end, with lights and decorations. But the men had finished at dinnertime today.

Past the warehouses and wharves. Once, Mr. Hegarty had been a nightwatchman on the wharf. That was when the ships had docked, years ago. There were no ships now.

Across the last bit of the empty lot. Jacko's ears twitched.

Home.

Christmas Eve. The wind blew down alleyways, across the dark wharves, smelling of rain and river. No snow. No star. But Christmas Eve isn't often like the stories.

Mr. Hegarty reached home. There was a carrier bag on the step, with three wrapped-up presents inside, and a card. "To Mr. Hegarty and Jacko and Cat, a Happy Christmas, with love from Jo."

Jo and his family lived next door. But they had gone away that morning, to stay with his grandmother for the holiday. One day, they'd go away altogether. Everybody would. This was the last street. Mr. Hegarty didn't want to think about it.

Nothing inside the house had changed very much since he and Mrs. Hegarty moved in, newly married; and since Mrs. Hegarty died, nothing had changed at all. Mr. Hegarty wanted it like that, just as it was and had always been and as she had left it.

He kept it clean and put things away in the same old places and polished the windows and blackened the hearth and washed up in the stone sink and slept in the big brass bed.

And every Christmas, he put up the decorations, around the

pictures and over the mirror and along the mantelpiece, with a wreath of holly on the front door, just as Mrs. Hegarty always had.

It was very quiet. Mr. Hegarty went into the scullery to wash his hands, then fed Jacko and Cat, put the kettle on, made up the fire, and sat beside it. And Mrs. Hegarty sat beside him, smiling out from the silver photograph frame on the little table.

Later, the band came and played "Silent Night" and "Hark, the Herald Angels," under the orange lamp at the end of the street, and the man with the collecting tin came down to Mr. Hegarty's door and they had a chat. Then, they played one more carol, which was "In the Bleak Midwinter," because it had been Mrs. Hegarty's favorite, before they went away. But for quite a while, the strains of trumpet and tuba and cornet, "O Little Town of Bethlehem" and "While Shepherds Watched" floated faintly back to him across the wharves and the empty lot. Then, it was quiet again.

For the rest of the evening, while Jacko and Cat slept on the hearth rug, Mr. Hegarty sat in his armchair, thinking, as people do, of other Christmases, good and bad and in-between—but mostly good, for times past are golden in the memory to an old and lonely man.

At ten o'clock, he got up, and Jacko ran to the front door, and they went for their last walk, up the street and down again. There was nobody about, though some of the houses had lights on, glowing behind curtains, and two of them had Christmas trees in the windows.

And the wind still blew, down the alleyways and across the wharves and the empty lot, with the smell of the river on its breath.

Christmas Eve. Mr. Hegarty's heart lifted. It was still special, after all, there was no getting away from that. Then, he let Cat out, locked up, wound his watch, and went upstairs to bed.

Sometime after midnight, he woke again. At first, he didn't

know why. There was no sound, except for Jacko, snoring softly.

Then, there was something, a very faint, distant sound, not inside the house, out. Mr. Hegarty put on his slippers, went downstairs, and opened the front door.

Everything was still. It had stopped raining and the wind had died down.

The moon shone.

Jacko came pattering down the stairs and stopped beside Mr. Hegarty at the front door.

There it was again. Very faint. A mewling sound. Kittens?

Mr. Hegarty put on his coat and shoes and took the flashlight. Then, he went out of the house and across the empty lot, toward the church. Jacko ran ahead, ears cocked, tail up.

There were railings around the old church, but the padlock on the gate was broken. The sound was louder. Mr. Hegarty stopped. The moon came out again from behind a cloud. Jacko had trotted up the weed-covered path to the church porch and Mr. Hegarty could see him standing beside something, wagging his tail. So he went too.

Here, the sound was loud and clear and unmistakable.

Mr. Hegarty shone his flashlight.

On a ledge inside the dark, damp, cold stone porch of the church, stood a shallow cardboard box.

Inside the box lay a baby. It was very small, and wrapped in a scruffy piece of blanket.

"Now then!" said Mr. Hegarty softly. "Now then."

But then he didn't know quite what to do.

He and Mrs. Hegarty had never had any

children. Mr. Hegarty had never even held a baby. In his own home, there had been seven children, but as he had been the youngest, all the others had picked him up.

The moon went behind a cloud again, and the baby stopped crying and just lay. Jacko sat, waiting.

"Well," said Mr. Hegarty.

And then, because there was nothing else that he could do, he picked up the box with the baby in it, very gently. And as he did so, he remembered that it was not Christmas Eve any longer, but Christmas Day.

Then, carrying the box very carefully, he made his way slowly out of the church porch, and back across the empty lot, Jacko trotting at his heels. He couldn't hold the flashlight as well, so he put it at the bottom of the box, by the baby's feet.

Up the street, past the building site and the wharves and warehouses—empty and silent—toward the streets, and then the market, the shops, the lane. His footsteps echoed.

The pubs and cafés had long since shut. The last trains had gone, and there were no cars on the main road.

Mr. Hegarty walked on, stopping now and then to set the box down and rest his arms.

Then Jacko stopped too, and waited patiently.

The baby had gone to sleep.

From across the last square, beside the bit of park, Mr. Hegarty could see the lights shining out.

"Now then," he said. But then, just for a minute, he didn't want to go on, didn't want to let the baby go. He felt a strange, half-sad, half-angry feeling, like a knot tightening inside him. Whoever could have left it in a box, in a cold porch, at Christmas? He looked down at it again. But then, because he knew there was only one right thing to do, he crossed the road and walked up the drive to the entrance.

"Stay," he said. Jacko stayed.

Then, Mr. Hegarty went through the glass doors into the lighted entrance of the King's Hospital.

In the hall, there was a huge Christmas tree, and paper chains and decorations strung from the ceiling and all around the walls.

At the far end was a reception desk, with a porter behind it, and a nurse standing beside. Mr. Hegarty went up to them and stood, holding the box in his arms.

"I've brought a baby," he said.

In the next hour or so, a lot of things happened. The baby was taken away, and Mr. Hegarty asked to sit down and answer a great many questions, from a nurse, and a doctor, and finally, from two policemen. They brought him a cup of tea, and then another, with a pink bun, and asked him to sign some papers, and the whole time, Jacko sat without moving or barking, on the step beyond the glass doors.

But in the end, the nurse came back again and said, "You can go now, Mr. Hegarty. You must be tired out."

"Right," said the policemen. "We'll drop you off. Trafalgar Street, isn't it?"

Mr. Hegarty stood up. He was tired, tired enough to drop, and muddled and in a way, sad.

"No, thank you very much," he said. "If it's all the same to you, I'll walk." And he went slowly across the blue carpet to the glass doors, where Jacko was waiting.

"Come on then," Mr. Hegarty said. Jacko came.

He did sleep, just a bit, but it was a strange, restless sleep, full of odd dreams and noises.

When he woke properly, it was just coming light. Gray. Damp looking. "Happy Christmas, Jacko," Mr. Hegarty said. Jacko hardly stirred.

He was going to make a pot of tea, and then open his present from Jo. But, as he washed, he knew that he wouldn't, not yet. Knew that he would have to go there first, straight away, because the baby had been on his mind all night, and he couldn't settle until he'd made sure about it.

He let Cat in, whistled to Jacko, and crossed the street, all over again, in the same direction as before.

And as he walked, he wondered. Whose baby? When? How? Why? What would happen to it now?

He hadn't even found out what it was, girl or boy, hadn't liked to ask.

The hospital looked different in the early morning light, larger, grayer, somehow less friendly.

But he left Jacko on the step again, and went in, down the blue carpet.

After he had explained, they left him, sitting on a chair in a corridor. The hospital was still quiet, but not like the night before. He could hear doors banging and the elevator going up and down. Perhaps they would bring him a cup of tea again. He always had one as soon as he got up. He was missing it now.

But it didn't really matter. He'd had to come.

"Mr. Hegarty?"

Mr. Hegarty stood up.

"Would you like to come with me?"

Through doors. Down a corridor.

"I'm sure you'd like to see him, wouldn't you?"

Him. A boy then. Yes, that was as it should be.

"He's fine, thanks to you. But if you hadn't found him . . . "

They went down more corridors. Around corners. Through doors. Stopped.

"You'll see that we've done something special," she said.

"We always wait for the first baby born in the hospital on Christmas Day, but there hadn't been one yet. And besides, we thought that your baby was the most important one here today. Come in and see."

There were babies in small cribs. Through a glass window, he could see beds.

"Look, Mr. Hegarty."

At the end of the room, on a small, raised platform, stood a crib, draped and decorated, under a canopy. Hanging above the canopy was a star. "The Christmas crib," she said. "Only used once a year. Today."

Mr. Hegarty went a step closer. Looked down. And there he was, the baby from the cardboard box in the dark church porch, the baby he had found and carried here with Jacko. The Christmas baby.

For a while, Mr. Hegarty didn't speak.

Then he said quietly, "King of Kings. That's who he is. The King of Kings." And went, smiling, out of the nursery.

They did find him a cup of tea, and a breakfast too, and a plate of sausages for Jacko, and said they would be letting him know what happened to the baby, when there was any news.

"And you'll be welcome to come and see him you know," the nurse said. "Any day."

"Thank you," Mr. Hegarty said. "Thank you very much. I should like that."

And then he went home, with Jacko trotting beside him, through the quiet early streets of Christmas morning.

Lanterns across the Snow

Preface

Last night, the snow fell. And then I began to remember. I remembered all the things that I had forgotten. Or so it had seemed. But not forgotten after all. They were all there, stored away like treasures.

Last night, the snow fell.

The sky had been darkening all afternoon, growing grayer and grayer, and swelling with snow. It must have been cold, too, bitter cold. You could see that it was cold. In here, I am never cold; there is always a small fire, even in summer. It's a small room, and rather dark, but brightened by the fire. The fire is quite enough.

I sit by the window until it is dark—every day. And so I *saw* the cold, the air freezing.

There is a tree outside, one tree. Its branches are bare now. They bow down just beside my window, and the birds come—a sparrow, a robin, a blue tit, quick, quick, quick. And there is one bush, set against the wall, all scattered about with winter flowers, like bright, bright stars.

Beyond this window, where I sit, there is a little backyard. With my tree, the flowering bush, the little birds. And I can look up between the houses and see the sky.

Last night, the snow fell, and then I began to remember. There is no one else left now, no one who remembers it all. Mother and Father are long dead. And brother Will, gone for a soldier, brother Will dead, too.

And Nancy in the rectory kitchen; and Sam Hay, who whistled through the gap in his teeth and put up the swing for me on the apple tree bough in the garden. And m'lord at the Hall, and his lady, and their pale-faced, pale-haired daughter whose frock I so envied, and whose eyes were the color of sea-washed stones, and who said to me, that Christmastime, quietly in a corner, "I am a disappointment to them, because I am not a son."

I told my mother, who frowned. "But *you* are precious," she said.

And old Betsy Barlow with one leg. Pether the churchwarden, and Mr. Vale the usher, Father's right hand.

And his curate, with the bobbing Adam's apple, and a new, new wife who smiled at me, and took my hand beside the Christmas tree, and smiled again—at Father, at Mother, at the curate, at brother Will, but spoke not a single word. And died, the next year, with her daughter Rachel, in childbirth. And the curate went away.

They are all dead, now.

And those from the village who came to church. And those who did not—but Father cared for them all.

I remember the great, bleak, brown-turfed Dorset barrows, with the buzzards soaring and circling above. The tiny cottages dark with smoke and crowded with children. The servants at the Hall, crammed into cold attic rooms, never having a space for themselves or hot water to wash in. The old men and women with thin hair and thin legs, and bent backs and no teeth, sitting on steps in the sun, or snug on wooden benches beside the fire, content among the washing and the bubbling stoves, and their children's children's children. Or alone, in our village, or the next village beyond, or tucked away at the end of forgotten lanes, and never a soul went by. But Father would go, and take us with him. "They should see for themselves," he said.

There is no one else left who remembers.

But last night the snow fell. And I remembered. I will write it all down, now, before it's too late, too dark. For I am the last to remember.

I remember the days at the turn of the year, with the first buds pricking on the blackthorn hedge, and bending down to find a celandine between the blades of grass; remember the scudding sky and the hares running and racing across the hills, and Will after them, far ahead of me, and Tip the terrier bounding beside; remember the swing, up, up, up, until I felt I would touch the floor of heaven.

Remember the haymakers' bent brown backs, and the great tired horses hauling the wagons home with their golden load, and the men's voices calling to one another, down the lanes in the last of the light. And we stood beside the gate to watch them pass.

Remember the tops of the elms in

the churchyard, being tossed by the winds of October, November, and the night one tree was brought down and lay like a giant, dead and fallen to earth, all jagged and ripped from its roots; and all the next night, the wind still roared and howled, and moaned and prowled around the house, rattling the latches, crying at my window to get in, so that I ran in fear to Will.

"Ghosts, ghosts! Ghosts in the graveyard."

But, "Hush, hush. Don't dare to wake Mother and Father. No ghosts, no ghosts," Will said.

"Yes! Oh, yes!"

In a grave in the churchyard, beyond the window, we had two brothers. Dead, long dead.

"The wind. Only the wind," said Will.

For never did winds blow as strong as they blew there, rushing across Ladyman Barrow, bending back the trees. It seemed to be the gathering place for all the winds of the world.

I remember.

I remember that we felt rich, *were* rich, when so many were poor. That our beds were soft at night, when the Son of Man had no place to lay his head, Father said, and others only the hard ground on which to sleep. That we were loved, when others were not; that we were warm, when out in the dark night-fields, the sheep and the cows, and the fox and the hares were all cold, and birds had been found with their feet frozen to branches. The pond and the ditches, the stream that flowed through the woods, turned all to ice, and stayed frozen and still for weeks and weeks on end. Forever, that winter seemed.

And out in their hovel, beyond Ladyman Barrow, an old man called Roberts and his poor, blind wife, died of being hungry, and cold, and ill, and alone. And Father never knew, not until too late.

And he wept—our father, so proud, and respected; our father, gray and stern and upright, wept and raged, and pounded his fist, and cried to heaven for vengeance. "Remember this," he said, "oh, you remember."

Last night, the snow fell. And I began to remember.

Remember joy and sorrow, nights and days, summer and winter and fresh, sweet spring; remember the tall old house, and the swing on the apple tree bough. The years roll back to reveal my childhood, set in a magic circle, bright, bright, before the dark.

I sit here beside the window that looks onto the little backyard, and the tree, with the birds on its branches, and the bush, starry with flowers.

November, December.

And above, between the houses, the sky.

Last night, the snow fell. And then, I began to remember. Spring days and summer days, autumn and winter. Father and Mother, and brother Will. The house and the church, and the grass and the graves between. The days of my childhood.

But I remember that Christmas best of all . . .

Christmas Eve

"Christmas eve," Fanny said. "Christmas Eve." As if saying it aloud would make her better able to believe it. "Christmas Eve," and she watched her own breath puff out like pale smoke in the cold air of her bedroom and turn to a fine mist on the windowpane.

Christmas Eve was the best of it all, the waiting and laughing, the sense of excitement through the house, like one of Nancy's black pots kept simmering. She thought of the rest of the day, and the evening to come, and saw a gleam of brightness cast forward from the blazing gold of Christmas Day, lancing toward her like the light streaming under the crack beneath a half-open door.

Christmas Day, Fanny thought, is like the room beyond that door, a bright, bright room, an Aladdin's cave of treasure; the tree with its candles and the banked-up fire all glowing, and the pile of shining presents, and the Christmas table, heavy with good things, the smells and the laughter and the love and, oh, the bright brightness. But for now, she was standing just outside, in the waiting room, and the light from the room that was Christmas Day just reached her, just touched, and she could feel her heart beat very fast.

She was nine years old. She could clearly remember last Christmas, yet it might have been a thousand years ago, it lay so far in the past, beyond the dark days of early winter, beyond the lingering days of autumn, beyond the summer, too; the heat and the flowers and the running about with petticoats all hitched up over bare brown legs, and the weeks beside the sea. In August, Father took over a parish near Lyme where the churchyard and the rectory garden sloped down to the path that led to the cliffs and the beach and the wide, wide bay. Brother Will had scrambled and climbed, and picked away for hours at the loose shale of the cliffs, digging for fossils. And finding them, too, chunks of blue-gray slate that opened like little hinged boxes to reveal the ammonite hidden beneath, coiled and ribbed like a snake. On the shingle were thousands of pebbles, and in among these they found treasures, tiny insects and animals, pressed into the hard stone, dead for a thousand years, Will said, and frail as paper shavings, but quite complete.

And they ran and ran across the great arc of the bay, and the soles of their feet left watery moons on the sand, and the sky had been so blue, so blue, but darker where it merged with the sea. They had woken each morning at dawn, to creep from the house and down the cliff path, and where their hands and legs brushed against the grass clumps, butterflies flew up in puffs and fluttered out into the air, white, primrose, and marvelous blue. Like angels, Fanny had thought, or like the souls of good people. But she had not said, only run faster, slip-slither down the last few yards after Will, and then onto the open beach, with the sea far out and glittering in the early sun, and the sand and the shingle pale, and the sky without clouds. And no one on earth but themselves.

Oh, glory, glory! Fanny had said. And lifted her arms and spread them wide, and danced; then run, toward the gold and silver of the sea. Oh, glory, glory!

Last Christmas was beyond that, beyond the whole of the summer and all the days of spring and another winter. She remembered everything about it, now it was so close again, was almost here . . . If she reached out her hand far enough, stretched and stretched with the tips of her fingers, she would reach it.

She stood at the window, looking out. Christmas Eve; and the snow fell like goose-down.

Her room was at the top of the tall house, seventy stairs to the landing, and the last flight was steep and narrow and wound around. Will's room was farther down the narrow passage, and on the way there was a window, but it was placed too high for Fanny to see out. She could only look at a patch of sky, not even at the tops of the trees, elms and Scots pines, that stood beside the church. But her own window looked down on the garden and graveyard beyond and the path that led to the small side door set in the wall of the church itself.

It had been snowing all day. It lay, softly piled over the earth, and outlined the curve of each gray gravestone and covered the flat tops of the chest tombs like quilts. The ledge outside her window was fat with snow. The church roof, the church porch, the bushes, and the yew trees that stood like statues in skirts were soft with snow, and the sky was gray as a wolf's coat, and still it went on snowing.

Behind the church lay Ladyman Barrow, that wild, wild, open place, of strange sounds and keening winds and rare bird cries, furze and heather and scrub. Narrow paths crisscrossed this way and that.

You could be lost and wander for hours, days, out on the Barrow; you could die of thirst and heat and confusion—lie down on the rough ground and gladly die there and never be found till your bones were white, Will said. Fanny was afraid of the Barrow, though Father walked across it for miles, on his visits to people who lived beyond. He strode out there, summer and winter, and knew every inch as well as those who'd been born beside it. He was never afraid on the Barrow, he said, never lonely or lost-feeling. God was always close. But it was that thought that Fanny did not like, though would never dare to have said.

On clear days, she could see the humped back of Ladyman Barrow from this window. On summer evenings, its outline was purple, the shadows between were lavender blue. On spring mornings, when the clouds raced, it dissolved into a pale mist, insubstantial, innocent, a place you might be happy on. Some days, it was only flat-gray, and dull, like a shape cut out of sugar-paper and pasted down onto the board of the sky.

Today, the swirling snow dazzled her, and the light was poor so she could not see the Barrow at all; for a moment, indeed, could barely see the church, a dozen yards away.

In the other direction, facing the rectory, lay the village, and to the west, the woods, acre upon acre of dense dark trees, a private and dreadful place that crept right down to the very edge of the rectory orchard, so that sometimes in the night Fanny woke to hear the squeal of small creatures, the cries of fear and the hunt and the kill, and the *shriek-shoosh* of an owl.

M'lord's keeper set traps in those woods—Catchpole, a man Fanny hated and feared, who carried the soft bodies of dead animals hanging down from his bare hands and dripping blood; and always a gun, broken beneath his arm. Catchpole came this way too often; he stopped by the kitchen door to talk to Nancy, or to leave his terrible gifts, a rabbit, a pair of pearly-gray wood pigeons, a bead-eyed pheasant.

"May the Lord make us thankful," Father said when they came to the table, and Fanny mumbled, and would have kept silent, and could have wept. But ate, all the same.

Suddenly, it had stopped snowing; the white world lay quite peaceful and still. And from down below, deep in the house, rich smells, voices calling, footsteps, a door closed. Christmas Eve.

Looking again from her high window, Fanny saw her father, tall and stooped and black as a crow in his black cloak, begin to walk across the deep snow of the churchyard, and from the gray stone tower of the church, the bell rang, *dong-dong, dong-dong, dong-dong.* Mr. Vale the usher, ringing for evensong. She could see the top of Father's head and his black shoulders, and as he made his way slowly through the billowed snow, a last flake or two came softly down to rest on him. There were deep pits made by his boots as he went, a line of them across the white of the snow. She watched him go diagonally between the graves, and then, as he always did, stop for a moment to look and bow his head, beside the place where her two brothers lay, the babies born and then dead long before Fanny ever was.

Then suddenly she wanted to go and be with him in the church, which by now would be decked out with all the green branches for Christmas Day. Wanted to walk out in the snow, and so she flew down the stairs like a bird, her feet barely touching each step, and the lower down she got, the richer and sweeter the smells were that wafted to meet her, plum pudding and baking, and oranges squeezed and cinnamon spice, and as she tumbled the last flight into the hall, the front door was flung open and in came Will, with Sam Hay, in a great white flurry of snow and cold air, bearing the log for the Christmas fire, and each of them draped in sheaves and swathes of green, their shoulders hung all about with branches and swags, of fir and spruce and ivy. They dropped them in piles on the floor, stamping their feet and blowing on fingers, and leaving snow to melt into pools on the clean polished floor.

Then out again, Will ahead. "Now for the mistletoe bough!"

"Oh, Mother!" she shouted. "Mother!" so that from the back of the house her mother came, rustle and busy-ness and seeming to be encircled with secrets in store.

"They've gone for the mistletoe bough!" and Fanny ran into the drawing room, up to the long windows that let onto the front lawn and the drive beyond, and from there she could just see Will, climbing, climbing fast up the oldest oak, while Sam Hay stood below and waited. "The mistletoe bough!"

But her mother had gone, back again into the farthest room of the house and her secrets, and Fanny knew why, because Will was climbing the great oak and their mother knew she must never prevent him, but nor could she ever bear to watch. Only Will would not fall; Will was like a cat. Will could climb anything.

From near the top of the tree, a sudden swift movement down to the ground, as the mistletoe bough fell onto the snow, and then, in a moment, another, a soft heap of pale green and milky white, gleaming slightly in the light that shone out from the window.

Fanny went back from the drawing room into the hall and stared at the Yule log and the mounds of glistening green, touched her finger to the hard red berries of holly and the pad of her thumb to a tiny spine. Then the front door came suddenly open again and, startled, jumping back, she felt the prick in her flesh and, looking down, saw already the bead of bright blood.

From below stairs, the crash of a tin pan.

At the kitchen table, Nancy, fat and floury and strong, stirred brandy into a bowl of dark and glistening fruit.

"Fingers out, I thank you, Miss Fanny Hart."

On the old chair beside the range, Nelson the orange cat stirred deep in his sleep and extended his paws and his claws, and settled softly back inside himself.

Fanny leaned on the table's edge, and half closed her eyes, sniffing up the sugary spicy fruity mincemeat smell, reached out a hand and began to roll a lemon that lay there, to and fro, to and fro, until, quite unexpectedly, it rolled away from her and fell *plop* onto the stone-flagged floor.

"Fingers *out*, Miss Fanny!"

Fanny ran.

"Child, child!" as she almost crashed into her mother, coming through the hall.

"May I go to Father? I want to go to the church by myself. I want to be out in the snow."

"Child, child!" but her mother was laughing. "Boots, then, and coat and bonnet and warmest scarf."

Oh, oh, hurry. Buttons and strings and hooks, all anyhow. Oh hurry, hurry.

"Perhaps, after all, Will had better . . . "

Fanny ran. Through the hall and down the dark passage between the coats to the heavy back door. Pulled it open slowly. And stood there for a moment, to catch her breath and grow calm before stepping out. And all the world was white. Click the door behind her, and then, oh then, into the snow. It creaked as she

moved through it, and blew up a little, dry as powder, and quite firm to the touch of her hand.

Oh, glory, glory!

She began to make her way across the churchyard with infinite care, wanting to disturb as little as possible of the perfect snow.

It was cold. It was absolutely still. Quiet, so quiet, she could hear the pant of her own breathing in, out, and the silky shuffle and squeak of her boots, pushing forward. She stopped. The air smelled cold. Tasted cold in her mouth. Above her head, the sky was clearing, and she could see a few stars pricking out between the parting clouds. There would be moonlight, then, and no more snow tonight. A bone-white, frozen, beautiful world.

She touched her hand to a gravestone and snow toppled off and fell on snow, soft as roses. Underneath, the rough gray stone, the lettering all worn away and moldy with moss; she liked the shape of the gravestones. And out here, among them, close to all those sleepers under the earth, she was not afraid. There were no ghosts.

Ahead, lights flickering out from the windows of the church. Behind, the golden glow from the windows of the house.

Christmas Eve, Fanny thought, and drew in her breath for joy.

Then she went on. But instead of making her own track any farther through the untouched snow, now she began to fit her feet into the deeper hollows made earlier by her father, and it was much easier, and somehow comforting, too. Her boots slid down easily, and then up again, though she had to lift her legs high, for her father's steps went so far down, down into the drifts.

She plodded slowly on, toward the building where her father was saying evensong, with only Vale the usher for company and to make the responses.

But *I* am coming now, Fanny said, and went on alone, in the last of the afternoon light, and the deep, deep snow, to join him.

Fanny knew that very early on Christmas morning, before even she was awake, Mr. Vale would come to light the big stove that stood at the back of the church. He would stoke it high, open up the flues, and pull down the grate, and stay there with it until everyone came for morning service and the building was as warm as he could make it, as warm as it could ever be made.

Which, in midwinter, was never very warm at all. But tonight, the stove was still dark and the church was as cold as death. It caught Fanny's breath and made her chest hurt as she breathed it in; the cold seemed to go deep, deep down into her bones and settle there.

She stood quite close to the door and looked down the little church to where the candlelight filled the chancel, beyond the beautiful stone arch. Around the arch were carved the running bodies of animals—a hare, a fox, a rabbit, a squirrel, a badger, a stoat, chasing one another, nose to tail, endlessly. And they ran in rings around the tops of the pillars, too. The stone arch was ribbed, with the curve of another, smaller arch immediately behind, and then another after that. Framed in it, the bare chancel, the plain altar with its pale wood, and one window, dark now, but by daylight, colored deep blue and sea-green, with at the center a crown of gold on the head of God, who sat enthroned among angels. Fanny loved the window. Loved the whole church, its gray stone and whitewashed walls, and high box pews, its coolness and plainness.

Now she went very quietly forward and when she got a step or two down the nave, stopped again and saw that the pulpit and the step, the arch and the pillars and all the window ledges, high up, had been decorated with swags and garlands and branches of evergreen leaves, holly, plain and glossy-dark and also the gold-edged kind, and all thick with berries. The ivy had been set in clumps and clusters, and then made to trail down the stone, and instead of mistletoe—for Father would never allow mistletoe inside the church, it was a pagan thing, he said—the ivy had been whitened here and there with flour, made into a water paste and then let dry, so that now it shone as if covered with milk-white flowers. Oh, pretty, thought Fanny, the green and the white, and the red of the berries. The prettiest thing.

From within the chancel, Father's voice rose, plain, tuneful, grave. "O Lord, save thy people."

And Mr. Vale the usher came back, sure, with the response. "And bless thine inheritance."

"Give peace in our time, O Lord."

And under her breath, Fanny sang, too, almost silently, the beautiful words she had known, it seemed, since the day she was born. "Because there is none other that fighteth for us, but only thou, O God."

Though in her heart she said, but I will fight, I will fight, and had a glorious vision of herself, slaying dragons and devils with the shining sword. For she was often puzzled by God, but she had never doubted for one moment the existence and power of the Devil.

But not here, not tonight. Tonight, she knew that no demon nor ghost nor evil spirit of any kind dared walk abroad.

If I look up to the roof, she thought suddenly, I shall see angels.

She moved into one of the pews and knelt down, and went on listening to her father's voice, comforted by it, and wondered and wondered about the strange story of Christmas.

"The grace of our Lord Jesus Christ, and the love of God, and the fellowship of the Holy Ghost be with us all evermore."

"Amen," said Fanny, clear out loud, and her voice rang, on the stone-cold air, so that her father half-turned his head, knowing now that she was there.

Then the candles were all snuffed out, and he came toward her, holding the lantern that threw flickering shadows up into his face, making it look lined and darkly hollowed out around the eyes and mouth, and sending his tall outline leaping up the wall. Fanny put her hand in his and felt the fingers stiff with the cold. "Child, child!" he said, and chafed hers gently in his own.

They went together to the church door and opened it, and saw that now there was the full moonlight falling onto the snow, and making it gleam white as bone.

"Christmas Eve!" said Fanny. "Christmas Eve!" Her father smiled. And they began to walk together, steadily home across the snow.

For the next few hours, she darted about like a restless bird, hopping here, skipping there, too excited, too unsettled, wanting the hours to pass quickly, yet wanting it to go on being Christmas Eve, the magic waiting time, forever.

They had tea, with cinnamon toast and raisin cake, before the fire in Mother's sewing room, and then Father went off to his study to write the sermon for tomorrow and his Christmas letters and Mother was busy again with her secrets, and closed the drawing room door tight, and Will was cross and only in a mood for teasing. So that in the end, Fanny wandered about by herself, upstairs and downstairs, in and out, and fretted, and thought, and puzzled. And yet she was happy.

At six, Mother came out to find her, and Nancy came up from the kitchen and Will down from the nursery floor, and for the next hour, they hung the green branches all about the hall and the holly wreath up in the porch, and trailed the garland of ivy, twined with ribbon, all the way up the banisters, and it looked as fine as it had ever looked. "Christmas Eve," Fanny said. And, dug out of his room to come and admire, Father stood beaming in the middle of the hall, and said, "Christmas. Blessed Christmas!"

After that, she went upstairs, and Nancy followed with the steaming water jugs, and the tin bath was set out before the nursery fire.

"Christmas Eve," Fanny said, and shivered, in spite of the heat of the water. "Christmas Eve!"

Downstairs again, then, she behind Will, and her long white nightgown tickled her legs and the lambskin slippers were snug around her feet. She went slowly, stair by stair, holding back and spinning out the golden moments. The hall looked suddenly quite different in its garlands of green; a strange, new place.

The door to the drawing room was still tightly shut. Silence. Fanny stood, holding her breath. Then, from below stairs came Nancy, and Kate the scullery maid, in best black and without their aprons, hair scraped back, faces solemn, strangers all at once.

On the wall, the gas jet spurted and the flame flared within the brackets, the holly and ivy were dark and gleaming softly.

And then, oh then, the double doors were flung open, and there in the long drawing room, beyond the lamps and the flames of the fire, the Christmas tree, tall as a steeple, and covered with candles like stars, with holly berries and with little oranges that were stuck about with cloves and hung upon scarlet ribbon. Fanny thought she might faint quite away with the joy of it, and she touched her hand quickly to her breast in a moment of fear that her heart had actually stopped.

Then, quietly, in they went, to where Mother stood smiling, and Father, too.

"Oh, beautiful," said Fanny, and gazed and gazed at the tree in its glory. "Oh, beautiful."

They sat around the fire, Fanny on the low stool, with Father in the wing chair, and Nancy and Kate just a little outside the circle, stiff and straight-backed, and the logs blazed up bravely, banked to the back of the grate, and the applewood smoke smelled sweet as sweet.

"And it came to pass in those days that there went out a decree from Caesar Augustus that all the world should be taxed. And all went to be taxed, every one into his own city. And Joseph also went up from Galilee, out of the city of Nazareth into Judaea, unto the city of David, which is called Bethlehem. To be taxed with Mary his espoused wife, being great with child."

And silently to herself, Fanny said the words as her father read them, and they sounded as beautiful as music to her, and just as strange, too, simple, yet infinitely difficult, as close and familiar to her as her own name, and yet far remote.

"And she brought forth her firstborn son, and wrapped him in swaddling clothes, and laid him in a manger; because there was no room for them in the inn."

And the brightness and the warmth from the fire, and the blaze of the candles from the Christmas tree, danced in front of Fanny's eyes, and the room seemed to be filled with a great blaze of light, as if it were one of the rooms of heaven, and Fanny's limbs felt leaden with sleep, and her head light as a dandelion clock that might be blown away, puff, from its stalk and float, float, off on the air.

"But Mary kept all these things, and pondered them in her heart."

Yes, thought Fanny, oh yes. And then listened to the silence that fell suddenly on the room as her father finished the reading.

She scarcely remembered going upstairs to bed at all—there was just a blur of faces and voices, firelight and candlelight, and the sensation of her own tiredness. The stairs to the top of the house had never seemed so many.

She awoke, quite suddenly, and lay, not moving, for several moments, wondering what sound she could have heard, what might have disturbed her. Then, she thought that she *did* hear a sound, very faint, not from within the house, but from somewhere outside and far away.

Fanny listened and listened. Nothing. Silence. She slipped out of bed and went to the window, and shivered, for the room was very cold.

When she drew back the curtains, she looked down on a magic world, gleaming white under the moon, with every line of the church roof and the church tower, gravestone and tree and hedge and wall, softened and blurred. The moonlight was very bright, and the sky was thick, thick with stars, glittering like pinpoints.

For a few seconds she stood stock-still there, looking, looking, and feeling the strange feeling that she might be entirely alone, the only one left alive in that cold, quiet, beautiful world.

Then, from a distance away, again she heard something, a voice perhaps, coming on the wind and, looking beyond, past the church to the fields, she saw them, a line of lights, like stars or glowworms, or fireflies, bobbing about, drawing very gradually nearer. She pushed open her window, so that its edging braid of snow toppled and fell, far down, and a little of it puffed back into the room, and drifted to the floor.

The air smelled sharply of frost. Fanny leaned out a little way, and felt it so cold it burned the skin of her face.

And then, she heard their voices much more clearly, a word or two passed down the procession now and then, and the lanterns, held high, came steadily nearer, until soon she could distinguish them more clearly, though they were all muffled up in greatcoats and leggings, boots and scarves and caps, against the cold.

"The carol singers are come!" Will said in a low voice, but still it made her start. He was standing in the doorway in his nightshirt. Fanny could see his eyes round with excitement.

"They've come, Fanny," and he moved to stand beside her at the window and watch as they made their slow way toward the rectory through the deep drifted snow, ten or a dozen of them, men and boys, all from the village and thereabouts, and carrying their instruments under their arms, or across their bodies, and every one with his own lantern, though they could not have needed them in the bright moonlight, except for decoration.

"Come on, Fanny," for the singers were making their way around to the front of the house. She took Will's hand and crept out and down the passage, and into the small box room that was scarcely used. Here the old baby crib was stored, and Father's trunk, lettered in black with his initials, and a strange case full of stuffed fish with glassy eyes, which Fanny hated.

Now, it was Will's turn to push up the window, and difficult, the sash was hardly ever lifted, and very stiff. By the time he had managed it, the carol singers were tuning their instruments, a note floating up now and again, from fiddle, or clarinet, or pipe.

Then, Seth Locke, the senior of them and leader, called for order and quiet, and gave the note and, suddenly, it began; the old tune came up to them through the clear cold air, and, closing her eyes, Fanny was transported by it and clutched Will's hand and squeezed it tight for sheer joy. And Will did not snatch it back to himself right away.

Joseph was an old man
An old man was he
When first he courted Mary
What a virgin was she.

Joseph and Mary
Walked out in Garden's wood
Where apples, plums, and cherries
As red as they grow.

They were deep voices, the voices of older boys and grown men, and the instruments were the homely ones, not harps and dulcimers and golden trumpets. Yet Fanny thought that they must surely be angels that sang and played, and she herself already, and quite certainly, in heaven.

When they reached the end of the long carol, they paused before striking up with another, and after that, they saw the bright beam of light fall across the snow as the front door was opened, and heard Father's voice, calling them to come in, and there was much stamping and bumping and banging of feet. Fanny and Will crept down inch by careful inch, so as not to make the stair boards creak, and sat on the step, high above the hall. And listened again as the men sang the wassail, and Richard the Carrier gave them a merry Christmas. After that, laughter, and the smell of hot pies, and the chink of the tankards of mulled ale as the tray went round.

Peering through the banisters, Fanny could just see the tops of their heads, and a glimpse of Father's arm, and the garlands of greenery all around. And if her mother, glancing up, caught sight of her, if she did, she looked away very quickly, and moved back a little, and did not say or do anything about it at all.

The carol singers gave one more verse, and then they were going, calling good night and wishing a happy Christmas over and over again, and Will touched her hand to go back upstairs.

I am not tired at all, Fanny thought. I shall never go to sleep now, for now it is almost Christmas.

And lay in her bed in the white moonlight, eyes wide, straining her ears for the last faint voices of the carol singers coming back to her across the snowy fields.

Now, it is almost Christmas, Fanny said.

And slept.

Christmas Day

Oh, the joy of waking, and remembering at once that it was Christmas morning. It was still only half-light, but because of the white radiance of the snow there was a brightness in her room, and Fanny could see perfectly well. She scrambled from her bed, and ran to the window and looked outside, but she could see nothing for the ferns and whorls and delicate tracery of frost on the inside of the pane. She touched her finger to it and it burned with the cold, and the air was cold, too, so that she dived back at once into her bed.

And then, oh, the joy of seeing the stocking hung on the bedstead knob and the bumps and bundles pushing out in all directions; and the pleasure of pulling out first this and then that, very gradually, carefully, heart racing with excitement, of looking and feeling and stroking and squeezing and guessing—of finding, finding a book, full of wonderful colored castles and silvery towers, and mythical monsters and princes and princesses, elves and goblins, winged beasts, fiery dragons; of finding a rainbow of wax pencils and a frieze of dolls made out of card, with clothes for them made of paper; finding sheets of scrap pictures of cherubs, and a wooden top that spun in a glorious arc of color when she twirled it between her fingers; and a very small wooden horse, with real hair for its mane and tail, and the packet of candy wrapped in golden paper and the red apple and the orange, orange tangerine, and the handful of warm brown nuts.

Fanny laid out her presents in a row upon the counterpane, and touched, and gazed, opened the book, and closed it again, stroked the mane and tail of the little horse. Then she heard Will come, bumping and banging along, with his hands full of ships and soldiers and a jointed clown on a string that you jerked, and a slab of butterscotch. Oh, the joy of its being Christmas! Of tumbling down the stairs to venison pie for breakfast, and real yellow cream on the bowls of porridge.

Then Father went ahead on his own to the church, and there was all the dressing in best coat and bonnet, and after she was quite ready, or so she thought, her mother went quickly away, and came back from her little sewing room with a brown paper parcel.

"A happy Christmas, little Fanny." Inside, the most perfect, gray fur muff on a shining, silver-gray cord—made out of a collar Mother had had on a coat worn before she was married.

Fanny put the cord of the muff carefully around her neck and slipped her hands into either end. It was like being close to the warm body of some still-alive creature, and her fingers met there and clasped together tight.

They were to walk, not across the churchyard from the back

door, but out at the front and around the path, as was only proper as the rectory family, on Sundays and festival days. The snow crunched under their feet, and everywhere, the sun caught on a million beads and drops of hoarfrost and threw off a million tiny rainbows, intensely bright and glittering. On the gate hung a spider's web, infinitely delicate, and stiff as frozen lace, with the spider itself frozen into the heart of it. And on the hedges and trees, and fences and posts, were the seams of snow. By the lych-gate, there was a robin on a yew branch, and in the way of robins, it kept company beside them, hop-hop, half a yard away over the snow, its breast red as a soldier's coat, its eye bead-bright.

And there was everyone else coming to church, and the carriage bearing m'lord and m'lady, with the poor horses slithering and sliding on the frozen road; and old people walking very gingerly, and children skipping, and breath pluming out, white as woodsmoke, on the cold, cold air.

And "A happy Christmas to you! Oh, a happy Christmas!"

Inside the church the stove roared and blazed, but it still felt bitter chill, and they could not sit close to the warmth either, the rectory pew was right at the front. Fanny tucked her hands deep into her muff and moved closer to Mother and then stuck out her legs, to admire the shine of her black button boots, and held the muff rather high, so that it might be seen. And Will, so proud in his best, stiff collar, would not catch her eye.

Father's sermon was about the real love and peace of Christmas. "Peace in your homes. Peace in your hearts." But privately, Fanny thought peace a very dull thing, and her mind wandered away from Father's words, and she puzzled again about God, and whether, if she turned her head very quickly, and without any warning, she might catch a glimpse of Him, before He ducked out of sight.

O come ye, O come ye to Bethlehem,
Come and behold Him,
Born the King of Angels . . .

Oh, yes, angels, oh, angels. That was all right again. She was quite at home with angels.

As always, she felt suddenly shy, standing by outside the church porch at the end of the service, while Father gave greetings to everyone, and being stiff in her best clothes, all unlike herself. But then, a great joy spurted through her as she looked around, at the beauty of the white snow, with its sheen of frost gleaming so bright under the morning sun that it hurt her eyes, and at red cheeks and bright eyes, at smart bonnets and cheerful faces, so that she wanted to dance and sing and shout, "Oh, glory, glory!"

Until she looked across the churchyard at the gravestones that leaned this way and that, and at the gray stone marking the place where her brothers lay—Edmund Charles and Arthur Frederick. And a picture came into her head, of them lying small and stiff and infinitely cold under the piled up earth and snow, and of all the sleepers buried here, dead, so long, long dead. It troubled her; she wanted to question it, and for a few moments a shadow touched her, and she felt far away from all the people talking together, smiling, nodding, wishing a merry Christmas.

After that though, the going home, and Will made a snowball and threw it at her back—but only gently, and when Mother spoke to him, it was not very sharply so that he only went on grinning. And they reached the house in time for everyone else arriving—the curate, who had been taking the early service out at Sawley, five miles away; and his new, new, smiling wife; and Uncle Jack, Mother's bachelor brother. And in half an hour, Sam Hay came over from Highwood Starrup, in the pony trap, with Grandmother Fairfax wrapped in rugs.

And then the Christmas table, with its snow-white cloth and polished glasses winking in the light, and the handsome, best silver that made Fanny clap her hands and laugh. And on the sideboard, a white dish on its stand was piled high with fruit, green and gold, purple and orange, yellow and red, and another held nuts, and a third sweetmeats, sugared almonds, and egg-yellow marzipan, and jellies covered in sugar crystal. Then they all sat down and the food came, smelling of richness and savory juices, and steaming hot.

The skin of the roasted fowl was crinkled and golden brown, the gravy ran like a thick, dark river; potatoes were fluffed up in the dish like mountains of snow. Fanny felt her mouth pucker up with hunger as Father said the grace and carved the bird and poured out the glasses of purple-red wine.

Then Fanny caught Father's eye and he smiled at her, so sweet, so tenderly loving, so happy a smile, that she thought she might melt all away with happiness.

"Christmas," she said abruptly, out loud, "oh, it is Christmas!"

And everyone laughed.

When the pudding was borne in, its dark, moist, gleaming roundness licked about by the blue flame where Nancy had set the brandy alight just as she stepped in, they all gave a cheer, and Will even banged the back of his spoon upon the table, until he saw Mother's quick frown. Fanny crumbled up her slice very carefully, moving it about the plate until she found the shining threepenny piece and the tiny silver horseshoe; and the curate got the wedding bells, and Uncle Jack the bachelor button, and Will got the donkey, and turned red, and everyone laughed again. And in the middle of the laughter, the door opened and Nancy came

in, all anxious, and Mother looked quickly across at Father.

"They have found Seth Locke collapsed in the snow. They have carried him to his cottage," Father said gravely. And stood up. "I am sent for," and he went out, touching Mother's arm gently, on the way.

"Of course he must go," she said to them around the table, but for a time, they were all silent, eating quietly, and not liking to go back to being jolly, and Fanny's heart blazed inside her with rage, that God should have let Seth Locke be ill, and take Father away from the Christmas table. She wished that they were a different kind of family, undisturbed by such things. But at once, she bowed her head for shame, and thought only of the poor old man lying sick and cold in the snow, and was glad, glad that Father was such a man, and to be proud of.

After a time, Will spoke up and told them a very silly, funny joke about a donkey so that Mother would know he had not really minded about getting it after all, and then the curate took up, and told a silly, funny story—though not as funny as Will's, funny though—about two cross-eyed pigs, and when she looked across the table, she saw that Grandmother Fairfax had gone peacefully to sleep over her plate of fruit and nuts, and she caught Will's eye, and Will gave her a great wink.

So the meal was not altogether spoiled, and afterward they went into the drawing room, and had their stocking presents down to play with. Fanny went, with her paper doll, behind the big sofa and sat on the floor with her back to it, looking out of the tall windows onto the front drive, so that she would be able to see her father return. They would wait to open the gifts that were under the tree, Mother said, until they were all together again.

And so the time passed, but very slowly, and Fanny fell into a kind of trance, watching the dazzling snow and a blackbird that was hop-hopping about very close to the windows, looking for food, and now and then the branches of the fir tree trembled as a slight breeze passed through them and dropped little pats of snow down with a plop and a flurry.

All at once, Fanny realized that her mother had come to stand near to her, and then she bent down and took hold of Fanny's hand and smiled.

"When will Father come back?"

"He will stay as long as he is needed."

"Yes."

And her mother came and pulled over the low stool and sat companionably down beside her, then, and took up the doll. And they stayed together, admiring the paper clothes, the fur-trimmed cloak and bonnet, the lacy dinner gown, and the great brimmed hat, covered in flowers and swathed with net, that Fanny could fit onto the doll as she wanted, with tabs, and Mother helped her to change the outfits and they both laughed a good deal. Behind them, Will and Uncle Jack and the curate argued and contradicted one another over the way the rigging should be threaded on a wooden ship, and Grandmother Fairfax told a long, long tale of India to the curate's smiling wife.

And then, suddenly, the banging and scraping of boots in the porch, and the front door opening, and Father was back.

Fanny got up and ran to him. And then stopped short, seeing his serious face, and she knew. And her mother glanced at him, and knew, too. "Oh," said Fanny softly, "*Oh!*" and felt tears of rage, rage and bewilderment and sorrow, for it was Christmas Day, it was Christmas Day, and nothing should be allowed to happen to spoil that. But it had.

"Seth Locke has died," she said out loud. Her father looked hard at her for a moment or two, then beckoned her to him as he went to sit in the wing chair close to the fire, and warm himself. Fanny stood stiffly, mutinous. "*Why* does God make people die? Why, *why* Father?"

There was a silence in the bright room.

Fanny had loved Seth Locke. He had had not a single hair on his head, and only one or two teeth left in his mouth, and a skin like the surface of a cobnut, and thick arms like great tree roots, and he had often lifted Fanny up, to sit on the back of one of the farm horses, and even though he seemed old, he'd swung her up as if she weighed less than half an ounce to him.

"I sat with him," her father said quietly. "He was asleep and awake, very fitfully. In much pain. They had laid him on the bench close to the stove. But he was very cold. I found blankets and a coat to cover him, but he was still cold. Then his eyes closed and he didn't move. I could barely see his breath. I wondered . . . I knew it was not to be long."

Everyone in the room was still, Will and Uncle Jack at the table, and the curate beside his wife, and Grandmother Fairfax in the upright chair, with Mother standing behind her. And Fanny close beside her father, taut as a bow. Everyone listened.

"And then, quite suddenly, he opened his eyes," Father said. "He opened his eyes wide, and he sat upright easily, without any pain, and he gripped hold of my hand." He paused for a long time, and Fanny saw that his eyes had filled with tears, and his face was solemn with the memory of what had happened, solemn, and strangely joyful, too, for all that he wept.

"He said in a bold voice to me, 'I have seen the glory,' and then again, 'I have seen the glory.' And he laid his head back on the pillow. And he was dead."

Father looked around, from one to another, until at last his eyes rested upon Fanny.

"Thanks be to God," he said.

And there was not a sound in the room except the spark and crackle of the fire. Until the curate said, "Amen."

Then her father reached out his arm and drew Fanny to him. "And there was not only a death today, little Fanny, there was a birth, too, a baby born for Christmas."

I know, I know all about that, she wanted to say tearfully, all about the Christ child and the shepherds in the fields and glory to God in the highest, but Seth Locke has still died, and never, never will lead the carols again.

But then her father said, "Thomas Tumney's wife was delivered of a son, early this morning. I met some of the older children in the lane, sliding on the ice." He looked at Fanny. "A death and a new life."

Fanny did not answer.

"I must get together a basket of food for them," her mother said. "The Tumneys have little enough, heaven knows." For there were ten Tumneys, the new boy would make eleven children, and Thomas Tumney always ill since he fell off the hayrick three years before and could not work; they were the poorest of the poor.

"Shall we go and see the baby, then? May I go? May we go now, today, at once?" But her mother frowned at Fanny to be quiet, and she saw that Father was suddenly weary, resting back in his chair. And at that moment, Nancy came in with the tea tray, and Grandmother woke with a start, and Will knocked the fire irons over into the hearth with a great *clang-clatter,* and soon, soon, they would have the gifts from the tree.

For it is still Christmas, Fanny said to herself. It is still the very middle of Christmas.

It was not until much later, when she was gazing at the candles, freshly lit and blazing again on the tree, and the beautiful little sewing case was in her hands, with its silver thimble and little pair of silver scissors, all her own, it was not until that perfect moment that she remembered.

Father had told them of Seth Locke's last words, and of the birth of the new baby. But he had not answered her question.

St. Stephen's Day

"The baby," Fanny said the moment she came into the dining room at breakfast time on the morning after Christmas Day. "I am going with Father, to see the Tumney's new baby."

Brother Will made a scornful, boy's face, and blew onto his spoonful of hot porridge with a loud noise, but bent his head down to eat quite quietly as their mother came in, and that made Fanny angry. She loved her brother, he was her best, her dearest friend, and every now and then, she hated him.

"Mama, *when* will Father take me to see the new baby? When shall we start out?"

But just at that moment her father opened the door and came in.

"*When* shall we go, please can it be at once, straight away after breakfast?"

Oh, the anguish of waiting, for her father only frowned very slightly, and said his grace, and sat down and watched Mother pour out his tea, sprinkled sugar very carefully over his porridge, and did not speak a single word. And brother Will kicked her shin beneath the tablecloth, but would not look at her, only away, out of the window, smiling a secret smile.

It is over, Fanny thought, Christmas is all done with and everyone is cross, the bright lights have been put out, and there is nothing but the days and days and days of January to come. And she felt a terrible, gray disappointment settle over and around her, and a lump in her heart, cold and heavy, as if it were a stone, and she stared down into her bowl, stirring and stirring the mealy lumps of pale porridge, no longer a bit hungry.

"Fanny is a crosspatch, Fanny has a black dog," Will said, and then again, twice, in a sing-song. "Fanny is a crosspatch, Fanny has a . . . " and Fanny felt her eyes prick with sudden sharp tears.

But then, looking up, she saw that Father's face was dark as thunder, and suddenly Will was silent and quite still and even seemed to be shrinking down inside his jacket. For Father's rage, if it ever broke, was to be feared.

After a moment, he turned his glance away from Will, to her.

"It is cold, Fanny," he said, "bitterly, bitterly cold. But the sun is shining and the sky is as blue as a blackbird's egg and quite without the smallest cloud, and the branches of the trees are lacy-white."

And he cut his triangle of toast into a smaller triangle, very neatly and carefully. Fanny watched him, and waited, waited.

"And today is the feast of St. Stephen. The day after Christmas Day."

And he ate a very small corner of the toast, chewing very slowly, and swallowing, and then taking a drink of his tea, and swallowing that, before speaking again. But this time, when he looked across the table at Fanny, she saw that his eyes were smiling and his mouth was just beginning to smile, too. "And I am a busy parson, in charge of a church and a wide parish, and today is a working day, Christmas or no Christmas."

And he reached over and chose an apple from the glass bowl of fruit, his hand hovering above this one and that one, before deciding, and taking the one nearest to him, and putting it on his plate and picking up the knife.

Then, his eyes were laughing, his whole face was crinkled with teasing laughter, and Fanny felt a great spurt of love for him.

"So that after I have eaten every morsel of my breakfast, little Fanny, I have to work. I must go out visiting. There is a poor widow to be consoled, and a very large family with a very new baby, to be cheered."

Fanny could hardly keep still on her chair for excitement but she sat on her hands, and pinched herself, and waited and, glancing sideways, saw that brother Will was scowling into his plate, with his dark eyebrows drawn tight together.

"I should very much like," Father said, wiping his mouth upon his napkin, "to have my daughter go with me for company. And the poor widow of Seth Locke and the poor wife of Thomas Tumney, and all the Tumney children, and most especially the brand new Tumney baby, would very much like to have her, too."

And he stood up, seeming very tall and straight. "Well, child?"

"Yes, oh yes? Yes, Father?"

"Are you going to keep us all waiting?"

Fanny jumped off her chair, so that she knocked it over. "Shall we go now? This morning, at once? Are we going already?"

"This very moment." And he clapped his hands to shoo her away; though she needed no shooing, was out of the room and across the hall and up the stairs. But as she went, she glanced over her shoulder, to see that Father had stayed behind in the dining room, to speak to Will, and because she was overflowing with happiness, she said, "Don't be angry" to him, under her breath, and willed the message to fly back and reach her father. "He didn't mean harm, oh, don't, don't be angry."

For it *is* still Christmas, she said, leaping up the stairs to her own room, to dress herself for the bitter cold morning, and the long walk to the village. It *is* still Christmas, after all.

When they stepped out of the front door, Fanny caught her breath with the shock of the most intense cold she had ever felt, and with wonder, too, at the beauty that she saw before her.

The world sparkled. The surface of the snow had frozen hard, and it shone like a faceted mirror, glinted and gleamed in the bright sunshine and the clear, cold air. As they began to walk, their feet made a ringing sound on the hard frozen ground, where a narrow path had been cleared down the drive, through the deep snow.

"Oh, beautiful," Fanny said, and held firmly on to her father's hand, letting her feet slide a little, this way and that. "Oh, beautiful."

And beside her, beneath the great cedar tree, she saw the blackbird, hop-hopping, as if it were on a spring, over the snow. And its eye, ringed around with an orange-gold rim, watched her.

After that, neither she nor her father spoke again for a long while, because once they had left the rectory drive and reached the lane, the snow, although it had been packed down in places, was still very deep, and walking through it was hard work. They had no breath left for talking. And the basket that Fanny was holding, which her mother had packed with good things for the Tumneys, was straight away too heavy for her, and she had to give it up for her father to carry.

They went very steadily down the lane that led between the high banks where in spring the primroses were thick and butter-colored, and cowslips and hundreds of white and purple violets grew, and on either side the hawthorn hedges were interspersed with trees, bare and severe and stately against the blue sky.

The air smelled of fresh, sweet coldness, and of snow too, though Fanny did not really understand how, for when she picked up a handful and brought it close to her nose, it smelled simply of nothing at all.

At the end of the lane, the stream emerged from between the banks, deep down in the ditch; Fanny peered and saw that it was opaque and frozen completely stiff. She wondered whether it had been like a living person, walking along quietly but gradually being slowed and slowed, as its blood ran thicker, more sluggishly, colder, through the veins, until at last, it could hardly move—and then, did not move at all; or whether, one moment the water had been rippling over the stones, flowing fast, as it always did, and the next, it had been seized by the cold and stopped dead in its tracks, so that somehow all the movement and light and liquidity was crystallized and held fast in the grip of the frost, exactly as it had been, when moving, only suddenly *not* moving, but stiff and still.

She dropped Father's hand and went closer to the bank. On either side, the grasses and the thick dead stalks of hogweed and cow parsley were powdery white and stiff, like sugar sticks. Closer to the water, whitened clumps of bog roses and mats of moss; higher up, the scrub and bracken arched up on itself, to form a roof, all pierced and torn through with holes.

Her father had stopped and was waiting for her, but Fanny did not move, only bent down, to where, on the grass, she saw a shrew. Its fur was frozen and its small, pointed face, with the long corkscrew snout, was frozen, too. In a moment of living, it had been taken by death, of cold. She picked up the body and held it in the palm of her hand. Its tail was thin and stiff.

And down in the ditch, and in all the hedgerow bottoms, she thought, how many other tiny creatures lay, frozen to death? And birds, wrens and tits, packed together in tree holes and under the eaves of privies, the smallest, frailest birds, unable to find any food or water.

She stood still in the bright, bitter morning, holding the shrew, until at last her father came back to her, and took the tiny creature and laid it gently down again between the clumps of frozen grass.

At the end of the lane, the ways forked, right to the open country that led up onto Ladyman Barrow. When they reached there, Fanny looked across to where it lay, white and softened now, merging gently into the other pillowed hills and fields around. Once the snow had melted, it would be brown again, dark, shadowed, even when the high summer sun shone full at the middle of the day.

Fanny loved, and was afraid of the Barrow, afraid of its bareness and openness to the wide sky, the strange sounds that were all about it, the way the wind keened there and the hawks and buzzards swooped and soared and then plunged suddenly down, and the way the shadows came behind and up and over to engulf you in abrupt chill grayness and make you imagine dreadful things. There were no trees, nothing to break the wide, bare brownness. But in summer, it was beautiful. The sun baked the earth, and made the furze give up a rich, pungent, herby smell, and the ground felt hot to your hand. She and Will were allowed out on the Barrow just so far, to where the white wooden signpost marked the crossing of all the ways. Then they would run off the dusty tracks, and plunge into the scrub and lie on their backs in the sun, while the butterflies fluttered all about their heads and over their faces, and you could reach out a hand and wait, very still, for one to come to rest on it, and tremble there, opening and closing its wings.

She loved the sandy-brown and buff rabbits that bumped ahead of them, before diving into their hundreds of holes. And once even there had been a snake, basking in the sun, its skin iridescent, its eye evil-bright. Will had poked it gently with the tip of a stick and it had uncoiled itself, fast as lightning, and slithered away and vanished.

Last year, they had found the remains of an old stone shelter, a cairn built by some heath-dweller or furze-cutter, long ago. Inside was only the bare earth for a floor; in the corner, an opening in the roof above a rough hearth where some peat, crumbling and blackened, still remained. Fanny had picked up a fragment, and smelled its faint, charred, acrid smell. Then, she had made a broom out of some bushy furze, and swept the hut out.

"We could live here," Will had said. "We could keep ponies and ride all day on the Barrow, and sleep on the ground at night in front of the dying embers, like gypsy people."

And Fanny had been ready to, at once. But then, a storm had blown up; low clouds shrouded the Barrow in a wet mist that clung to their hair and clothes like cobwebs, and then a wind had driven the rain in through the doorway and the window spaces, and down the chimney hole, soaking it all and churning the floor to mud. Then it had seemed a lonely, little, miserable place.

"Poor person who lived there," Fanny had thought as they ran and ran through the rain, for home.

The left-hand fork of the lane led toward the village, and here the snow had drifted higher than ever to one side, so that she and Father had to keep in file, close to the opposite stone wall, and Fanny's boots sank deep into the soft, cold drifts almost to their tops. But she felt bold and important, coming visiting with her father, and when first one and then another person saw them, and stopped to talk, she felt proud, too. She was there because Father had wanted her, for her company and because he felt that others would welcome her also.

Seth Locke's cottage was at the far end of the village street, beyond the pond and the horse trough, the inn and Ellen Rose's post office. It was one of three that were joined in a row together, and set back beyond a long, straight path that led up through the middle of the garden.

In summer, there were rows of giant hollyhocks on either side, with floppy petals all colored pale, like clothes that had faded from too many washings, Fanny thought. And in between the hollyhocks and sweet williams, the columbines and cornflowers and the net of small, frilled pinks were set creamy cauliflowers and purple cabbages, because Seth Locke had liked them there. They were as good as any proper flower, he had once told Fanny. That same day, he had picked her a little nosegay and surrounded it with cool damp primula leaves, and she had felt like a princess, carrying it carefully home.

Now she walked solemnly up the same path, whose small uneven bricks were treacherous with hard-packed snow, and looked at the billows of it piled over the earth of the garden, and thought of everything that had been growing and living buried deep and cold, and of poor Seth Locke himself, who was dead too and would never see his garden growing again.

Before they reached the cottage door, it had opened, and there was Seth Locke's daughter Flora, come across the winter fields from her own home seven miles away at Nune Abbas. And seeing her, with the dark cottage room behind her, Fanny felt suddenly overawed, and nervous too, so that she touched her father's hand for a second before drawing herself up, very tall and straight, anxious to do everything in just the right way.

Seth Locke's wife Mary was sitting on the wooden bench beside the fire, which was banked high and darkly smoking, not giving any warmth or brightness out into the cramped room.

Her face, when Fanny could make it out more clearly, was pasty and pinched with sorrow, and her eyes looked sore. She had on a best, shiny black dress with a long row of buttons, and bands of plain tucks down the front, and a clean apron over, and her hair was coiled around and around, tight as a braided bread at the back of her head.

Fanny stayed near to the door while her father went in and took Mary Locke's hand and held it, speaking to her quietly. She had scarcely ever been inside the cottage. Whenever she had visited Seth Locke, he had been outside in the garden, or the lane, in the yard behind the smithy, or on the road, leading one of the farm horses. Seth Locke hadn't been a man for indoors.

She started, realizing that her father was looking across at her, and then went forward slowly, and stood beside him. Close up, Mary Locke's face looked sadder than ever, her eyes watery but as though they were looking far away, and she knitted her fingers together in her lap.

Fanny felt her mouth go dry, and she licked her lips and swallowed. But then, thinking about how it was, remembering how Father had come home yesterday to the Christmas family, and told them of Seth Locke's dying, remembering Seth himself, and how she had liked him, Fanny bent down, and put her arms around Mary Locke, and hugged her as tight as she could, smelling the cupboard smell of the best black shiny dress.

"Oh," she said, and looked up into her face, "oh, I am truly sorry that Seth Locke has died, but I am truly glad that he had seen the glory."

And for quite a long time, she stayed, holding tight to the woman's hand, wanting to be a comfort to her.

Then, from behind, in the doorway, Flora Locke said, "Would you step up now, and see him?"

There was a silence until Fanny stood resolutely up, and looked at her father and at Flora Locke.

"I will go," she said in a clear voice. "Thank you, I will go up and see him."

"It is only to say good-bye, Fanny. *I* must, but you . . . "

"Yes," Fanny said, wanting to and not wanting to, but quite certain what she must do. "I will go with you."

Her father smiled at her and touched her shoulder, and then they followed behind Mary Locke and her daughter, slowly, slowly up the steep little twisting staircase, and into the bedroom above. Here, there was a bright white light from the reflection of the snow on the roof outside the high window, and Fanny saw that a great swag of snow hung down like a bee-swarm from the thatch, and attached to it were silken, transparent icicles, thick as reeds.

The bedroom was cold as cold, and very neat, with rag mats on the boarded floor. As they went in, Father seemed as tall as a tree, and had to bend so as not to hit his head on the beam. Fanny shut her eyes tightly for a second, and drew in a breath from deep down in her stomach, up and up through her whole body.

When she opened her eyes again, she was looking at the high brass bed that filled one end of the room, and at Seth Locke who lay there, pale as pale in the white light, on the white pillow, under the white, white sheet.

Behind her, Mary Locke gave a little sob and a sniff, but then, composing herself, went to stand beside Father while he said a prayer and gave them a blessing. And in the cold, cold room, Fanny began to shiver, and pressed her knees together and her elbows close in to her body and, hearing her father's voice, low and steady, thought suddenly, I shall remember this. I shall always remember.

Then she stepped forward, two, three small steps, and reached out her hand, and touched the folded hands of the dead man, and looked full into his calm face, so like it had always been to her, and yet so utterly strange.

"Good-bye, Seth Locke," Fanny said to him in a whisper.

And his hand was as cold as the coldest stone to her warm touch.

Although the Lockes' cottage had been dark downstairs, and crowded with heavy furniture, it had still felt strangely empty to Fanny, because of the death; and even when the four of them sat down and drank tea and ate small slices of plain seed cake, she felt there were dark corners full of emptiness all around.

Thomas Tumney's cottage was no bigger, it was a damp, dark little place, close to the pond, and set up against a high bank that dripped dank growth and creeper, and the front door opened straight onto the street.

But inside, there seemed to be not a single nook or cranny left vacant, every corner was crammed with children, while the range, a great wooden bench, a laden clotheshorse, and Thomas Tumney's couch—for he had not been able to go up the stairs since the injury to his back—took up the rest of the room. It was very hot as the fire in the range glowed red, and the room smelled of damp washing and children's bodies, and boiling bones, and the wet hair of the scruffy dog that lay on the rug. In the midst of it all, on the low stool, sat Thomas Tumney's wife, her hair springing out from its knot and standing up wildly all about her head; and beside her, in the low wooden crib, swaddled in old pieces of sheeting, the baby, born on Christmas Day.

As they went in, Fanny felt eyes watching her from every corner of the room, and, half-glancing around, saw faces peering out from behind the furniture. When they had come walking down the street toward the cottage, Tumney children had come out to meet them, inquisitive, large-eyed, but silent.

Fanny stood, feeling out of place and uncomfortable, but when her father looked at her, she went up to Tumney's wife, and set down the basket which they had brought, full of Christmas food and, below that, a layer of clothes for the baby, while on the very top, a crusty loaf of Nancy's bread, new baked that morning and wrapped in a cloth.

At once, the Tumney children came closer, to peer down into the basket, and lift the corner of the cloth, trying to see what was inside and, at the same time, staring at Fanny. They all looked very like one another except that some had red hair, like their mother, and others were dark, and they were dressed all anyhow in clothes that did not fit or belong. And Fanny felt suddenly angry that Thomas Tumney could not work, and so they had to be poor and wait for other people to bring them clothes and food, and ashamed that she had so much, clothes that were warm and bright and properly fitting to her and rooms that were full of space in which to be.

I shall remember this, too, she thought, remember the hot, crowded room and the smell of so many children and of the wet dog and the boiling bones, and the sadness on Thomas Tumney's face, lying on his couch.

Then one of the older children, the girl Eliza whom Fanny sat near to in the schoolroom, came up to the crib, and bent down, and gently lifted up the baby. She cradled him close for a moment, before moving back the clothes to show his face. And Fanny saw Eliza smile, with love and pride, and looked at the others who came crowding around, one to hold a finger, the other to touch the baby's face; she saw their gladness, the warmth of their welcome to him, and felt suddenly shy, standing outside their loving circle, until Eliza said, "Would you not like to hold our Christian?" and proffered the baby until Fanny took him very carefully, uncertain exactly what to do.

"Put a hand here—and crook your arm so—there, there!"

"Oh," Fanny said, and looked down into the small, delicate face, and wondered at it, at the faint violet-blue of the creased eyelid, and the rose-red of the pursed mouth, and the fine down of hair, red-gold in the light.

She put out a finger and touched the baby's hand, and at once the small fingers curled in and gripped her own, and inside the palm it felt sweetly damp and warm.

Fanny looked up and saw her father watching her from the chair he had drawn up to Thomas Tumney's couch, and she smiled at him, and at Thomas, and his wife, and the faces of all the children surrounding her.

"He is so beautiful," she said, and looked down at the baby again. "He is beautiful."

And for that moment, she did not feel sad nor sorry for them, only gladness, and a great, great envy.

She handed Christian back then, and sat down on a stool and, for a long time after that, she had to wait for Father, patiently, while he sat and listened, first to Thomas Tumney, and then to his wife, heard all their worries and fears, and then the story of their eldest daughter Rose, who was fourteen, and in service at Hestone Manor eleven miles away. How Rose had been ill all that winter, with fever and a cold in her chest, and how she had grown too thin and could not stop coughing all the nights, but was forced to sleep in an attic where the windows did not fit, so that the rain and wind and now the snow came in, and had to get up at five every morning to light the fires, and work in the dank scullery all day. And how two of her brothers had trudged through the deep snow on Christmas afternoon, to take her a gift and tell her about the new baby, for she had not been allowed any time off to come home herself.

When they got there, they had waited nearly a whole hour by the stable clock until, at last, Rose had come out to see them, though only for a few moments, and they had been frightened, she had looked so thin and pale and had coughed so badly. She had not been allowed even to take them into the back kitchen so they had all stood in the cold wind until she was called back for there was a big party of folk at the house for Christmas and she said everyone was needed to work. So Josh and Jonah had had to walk back home again without any food or a drink given.

"And that was Christmas Day," said Thomas Tumney's wife, in a low, sad voice. "And they all Christian people."

And, of course, Father had said that he would go there himself, the very next day, and see Rose, and fetch her to the doctor, and speak to the people at the Manor, about her being kept warm, and looked after properly, and his voice had been cold and hard with anger.

After that, Thomas Tumney had begun to talk again, telling a long tale of woe and misery. And all at once, the children were shooed outside, and they urged Fanny to go with them, and they made snowballs and slid about in the lane, and went to bang sticks on the pond to try and break a chink in the ice. But it was frozen deep, deep down as far as they could see, and it only chipped a little and bright, hard slivers flew up like glass.

By the time Father came out of the cottage and they set off for home again, Fanny's cheeks felt as if they were on fire in the coldness of the air, but it had been a very long time since her breakfast, and along the lane beyond the fork, her legs felt suddenly very tired, as if they would not carry her, and her head was buzzing. So then they stood in the shelter of the high hedge, and Father took a little paper package of muscatel raisins from deep in his pocket, and they shared them together, and rested until Fanny was quite ready to go on. And nothing, she thought, nothing, nothing, had ever tasted so sweet and good in her life.

But the best thing of all to happen that whole Christmas was still to come, and until they had reached home, and Fanny had taken off her outdoor clothes and washed her hands, and sat down to the luncheon table, not a word was said about it, it was the most complete and perfect surprise. Though as soon as she saw him, she knew that brother Will had a secret, his face was brilliant with it, he smiled and smiled, and kept looking at Fanny, and then at Mother, and smiling again, and shuffling and tapping his feet and nodding his head, until he was frowned at to be still.

But her mother looked pleased, too, Fanny thought, and full of the same private knowledge.

First, though, she herself had to tell, about the walk and about how she had gone to say good-bye to Seth Locke, and about holding the Tumney baby. And as she talked, and listened as Father talked, and ate her meat and drank her milk, tiredness began to seep into her limbs again; she felt as if she were being covered over with a thick, soft, heavy counterpane, and all their voices sounded farther and farther away.

Then, looking sharply at her, her mother said, "Time to tell" to Will, and Will sat bolt upright, and Father looked from one to the other of them, for explanation. And Will said very slowly, "While you were gone to the village, a message was brought."

Fanny watched his face intently.

"A message from m'lord at the Hall. And the message was an invitation to Mr. Hart, the rector, and to the rector's wife, and the rector's son."

He looked teasingly across the table at Fanny, and paused, and took a long, slow drink from his water glass, and set it down carefully again.

"And *even* to Miss Hart, the rector's daughter. Oh, imagine that!"

But Fanny felt too tired to be impatient with him. She just sat in half a dream, and saw the white world beyond the windows, and the blackbird as it went hop-hop-hop across the snow, and waited.

"We are invited to a party from six o'clock this very evening. At the Hall. An illuminated skating party on the lake, which has frozen hard as hard, with music. And refreshments. And all manner of delights!"

Then Will stood up and waved his hands in the air, and said, "And isn't *that* the grandest thing, little Fanny!" and then he came around to her chair, and pulled her off it, and danced her around and around, and Fanny saw how his eyes shone and caught his own excitement in spite of her tiredness, and let him jig her up and down the room, while Mother and Father looked on and smiled, at them, and at one another.

But then, Mother stood up and came over and took Fanny's hand.

"Bed," she said. "Sleep, if you are to be allowed to a skating party, *after dark!*"

And Fanny went with her very willingly, and wondered only if her legs would carry her to the top of the stairs. When she undressed, and slipped into her bed, she felt down to find that the hot stone water bottle had been put there.

"Wake me up," she said, watching her mother draw the curtains across to shut out the bright daylight. "Don't go there without me."

"No," her mother said, and bent to stroke Fanny's hair, "oh, no!"

And Fanny slept, and did not even hear her close the door behind her.

"After this morning," Fanny said, as she was doing up her coat in the hall, and her fingers were all thumbs and the right holes matched the wrong buttons, "after this morning, my legs felt so tired I thought they might never go properly again. But now . . . " and she did a few steps on the flagged floor, "now, I could run and run and dance and dance, and walk for a hundred miles."

"Only you won't have to walk for a hundred miles, or even for one," Will said. "And that is another thing you didn't know, but I knew."

"What do you mean? Oh, tell, Will, *tell* . . . "

But what Will did was not tell anything, but instead, he listened, and then said, "There!" And Fanny heard it too, a noise outside in the drive, the sound of wheels, and of stamping. "There!" said Will. "We are sent for!" and he flung open the door. And there, outside in the snow, stood the trap from the Hall, pulled by one of the gray ponies, and with Dorkin, the younger groom, at the reins.

Then Father and Mother, and Will and Fanny stepped out into the snow, and behind them in the hallway, Nancy and Kate came to admire, and to wave them off, and after Fanny had stepped up into the trap and had sat down, Dorkin tucked a rug around her. She looked up and saw that the night sky was pricked all over with bright, bright stars, and the moon was round as a pumpkin and pale as silk, and it shone full onto the snow so that they could see as well as in the brightness of day.

And as they set off, she pinched herself, in wonder that this was real and she herself a true and living part of it.

The Hall stood quite close to the rectory, at the end of a long avenue of elm trees. But tonight, they took the road that wound around away from the house, through a copse, and then out into the clearing to where there was a dip. And in the dip, surrounded by sloping grassy banks, lay the lake.

As they drew near to it, looking ahead, Fanny saw lights

flickering, yellow and white and green and red and blue, like a rainbow in the darkness, and then the lake lay before them, frozen, glittering, unearthly under the rising moon. And set all around it on poles in the grass were Chinese lanterns, and in other places, fires—logs set within iron hurdles, and blazing bright, and right on the edge of the ice were two great braziers, glowing like the smithy's forge, and sending showers of white sparks flying up into the night sky.

Already people were skating, in pairs and singly, and then m'lord and lady were welcoming them, and Mother and Father were thanking and talking and, catching her eye, Will gave Fanny a great wink of delight.

There were benches laid out with spare skates and boots, for any who had not their own, and, seeing the brightness and sharpness of the blades, Fanny hesitated, suddenly afraid of them, and of the great, shining expanse of the frozen lake. But Father and Will said they would take her between them and hold her up, and so they did. She went very carefully and safely around the edge, but in a little while, grew bolder, and set her feet down more firmly, one-two, one-two, and felt the cold air on her face, and heard the blades *hiss-hiss*.

Only it was quite difficult, after all, and cold, too; she could not skate for long, so they brought her back to sit close to one of the braziers, and watch Mother and Father skate off beautifully over the ice, with hands linked across.

Then came the music from the other side of the lake. The band, which had been setting itself up, began suddenly to play, and more and more people were arriving and taking to the ice, and they skated the quadrille and the lancers, and then there was a pause before the band played a gallop that got faster and faster, so that the blades of the skaters skimmed and flew and hardly seemed to touch the ice, and Fanny saw her mother go past with her eyes shining and her muffler streaming behind her. Some people were skating with torches, holding them up so that they flared and flickered, and made trails like fiery comets in the darkness.

And the colored lanterns swung and shone, and made bright watery pools of light on the ice, and the air was sweet with the smell of wood smoke and roasting chestnuts and it was cold, cold, and the sound of the music and the laughter, the calling voices and the *whip-whip* of the skate blades all began to swirl and dance before Fanny's eyes. It was as if the whole world was spinning and caught up in the movement of the skating and the beauty of the moonlight and the torchlight and the lantern light on the ice of the lake, and the snow-covered banks all around.

She thought she had never been so happy in all her life, never felt so joyful and light of heart, that there had never been such magic in the world, such wonder, such a Christmas.

And suddenly, she stood up and, in the snow, began to dance to the music, to hold out her arms to the lanterns and the glowing fires and the skaters, and her head was light and the earth spun like a top, and she looked all around her and then, at last, up at all the stars in the sky. And very quietly, in a whisper, she said, "Oh, glory, glory!" so that only she herself could hear.

"Oh, glory, glory, glory!"

And much later, riding home again in the trap, Fanny felt more wide awake than she ever had in her life, and as though she were seeing everything for the first time.

The fields were bone-white, and completely empty and still, and the gray coat and mane of the pony gleamed and the harness glinted now and then, and the trees arched over them as they drove

through the copse. And, looking up between their silver branches, Fanny saw the evening star, the brightest and strongest of all, and as they turned out into the lane, it stayed just ahead of them, to lead their way home.

AFTERWORD

LAST NIGHT, the snow fell. And then I began to remember. And today is Christmas Eve, and still it snows, and still I go on remembering, and the memories will keep me company.

I sit here, beside the window, and watch the snow, and the blackbird who comes and sits under the flowering bush, and after a while hops out farther, to find the food that I have thrown. The yellow flowers of the bush are dusted with snow, and the bare branches of the tall tree are outlined delicately in white. And I sit here, beside the window, and my lamp throws its light in a pool onto the ground below, but there is no snow so close to the building, the overhang of the roof above deflects it.

And all last night, and all today, I have sat here quietly and remembered. Remembered joy and sorrow, nights and days, summer and winter, in that perfect place.

I remember my room at the very top of the tall old house, and the view out over the churchyard, and the gravestone of my two dead brothers. Remember the stone church and the fields beyond, remember the woods and the lanes and Ladyman Barrow.

And Nancy in the rectory kitchen, and Sam Hay who whistled through the gap in his teeth. And m'lord at the Hall, and m'lady. Old Betsy Barlow with one leg, Pether the churchwarden. And Mr. Vale, the usher, Father's right hand. And his curate with the bobbing Adam's apple and the new, new wife.

Father, and Mother, and brother Will.

Last night, the snow fell, and I began to remember. Today it is Christmas Eve. And I remember that Christmas best of all, when I was nine years old, and the snow lay like a goose-down quilt over the earth, and I walked across the churchyard, through the deep, soft drifts, to listen to Father say evensong, by the light of the candles.

I remember the carol singers coming with their lanterns across the snow, and their voices, and the sound of the flute and the fiddle. Remember sitting on the stairs with brother Will, and our mother handing around the plate of mince pies in the hall below, and not looking up at us or noticing.

And in the kitchen the sweet, rich smells and the dark, dark fruit in the china bowl, and a cat on a cushion and a lemon rolling onto the stone-flagged floor.

Remember sleeping and waking in the thin, blue light of Christmas morning. And the great stove blazing in the icy church, and the brown savory skin of the roasted fowl, and the death of Seth Locke and the birth of Thomas Tumney's baby; and on St. Stephen's Day, the stiff dead body of the tiny frozen shrew, the feel of Seth Locke's hand to my warm touch, and the new, new baby in the crook of my arm.

And the skating with torches, and the great, great beauty of that snow-covered world.

I remember. For that was the last country Christmas. The next spring, Father was made a canon of the cathedral and we went away, away from the rectory and the little stone church, and the grave of our two dead brothers; away from the fields and the woods, the lanes and the stream and the ditches, and the great wide barrow. Away from the country to the city, where we were happy enough in another tall house, joined to a row of others and set in a narrow street, but where our life ever after was so very, very different.

And after that, it seemed, I left behind my childhood, that magic time, set within a circle and lit from within, so that the memory of it, coming to me down all the years, is golden as the light of a lantern falling across the snow.

Can It Be True?

Can It Be True?

It was Christmas Eve,
on the farm
in the fields
in the streets of the town.

It was Christmas Eve
and twelve of the clock,
when the message was heard
on the wind in the trees
on the air
underground
and humming through wires
and slipped into dreams.

Heard by the fox
slinking up to the hens
in their ark in the dark
and the worm, down, down,
and the wolf as it prowled
near the sheep in the fold.

Heard by the dog as it snarled at the cat
as it sniffed for the mouse
as it cowered in the hole in the wall
of the house, in its fright.
As, out of the alley
a hissing and spitting and yowling
Tom-fight.

It was heard by the owl
with blood on its beak,
and the shrew
in the ditch
and the general in bed and dreaming
of war
and the fierce lines of soldiers
on nursery floor.

Heard by the weasel,
the ferret, the stoat,
the terrified rabbit
the whale in the sea
and the whaler above in his boat.

And the huntsman,
tantivvy, tantivvy in sleep.
The hounds
and the hare
out there in the fields
where the frost hard as iron held
the earth in its grip.

Christmas Eve and twelve
chimed the clock
on the church
in the town
on the wall
in the hall,
when the message was heard.

Christmas Eve.

And can it be true?
And can it be true?
Said the fox to the hen and the hen to
the wolf and the wolf to
the sheep and the sheep to
the dog and the dog to
the cat and the cat to
the mouse and the mouse to
the owl and the owl to
the shrew and the shrew to
the general in bed.

Can it be true?
He said
in his dreams to the men in their lines
on the nursery floor, and the men
to the weasel and ferret and stoat,
and the whale to the man
with the gun in his boat.
Can it be true?
said huntsman to hounds,
tantivvy, tantivvy,
and the hounds to the hare
in the field
in the cold.

And can it be true?
When the message was heard.
Come and see for yourself.
So they left off their
fighting and hunting and chasing
and dreaming of war.

And they went:
the fox with the hens
and the wolf with the sheep
and the dog with the cat
and the cat with the mouse
and the owl with the shrew
and the men
and the weasel, the ferret, the stoat
with the rabbit,
and huntsman and hounds with the hare.
And the whale towed the boat
to the shore.

And halfway there,
through the fields, and the woods
and the streets of the town
came the snow.

Christmas Eve
and twelve of the clock
when they came to the stable
and saw . . .

It is true! It is true!
And knelt down.